Ragan's Law

Also available in Large Print
by Ray Hogan:

Man Without a Gun
The Yesterday Rider
The Doomsday Posse
The Peace Keeper
The Glory Trail
Pilgrim
The Doomsday Bullet
Lawman's Choice
The Proving Gun
The Vengeance of Fortuna West

Ragan's Law

RAY HOGAN

G.K.HALL&CO.
Boston, Massachusetts
1984

Published in Large Print by arrangement with
Doubleday & Company, Inc.

British Commonwealth rights courtesy of Scott Meredith
Literary Agency, Inc.

Set in 18 pt English Times.

Library of Congress Cataloging in Publication Data

Hogan, Ray, 1908-
  Ragan's law.

  1. Large type books.   I.   Title.
[PS3558.O3473R3   1984]   813'.54   84-12777
ISBN 0-8161-3622-X

For . . . CLAY GRADY

1
___

Cursing as his horse stumbled and went to its knees, Dan Ragan kicked free of the stirrups and leaped clear of his saddle. Around him in the closing night the ragged land was a turbulence of slashing sand, whirling, choking dust, and buffeting wind.

Landing on all fours and still clutching the gelding's reins, Dan pulled himself upright hurriedly and wheeled to do what he could for the horse. But the big sorrel, apparently none the worse for the fall, was already up. Legs spread, head lowered, he now stood trembling and patient in the blinding, savage blow.

Ragan had seen the storm coming—a great tan and gray wall sweeping in from the vast area known as the Panhandle, to the east—but had given it little thought. In the first place there was nothing he could do about it, and in the second there was the chance, he knew from experience, that it could change course, swing south or north or possibly even die off to become just another duster before it reached the trail he was following.

But it had not. Instead, as if determined to prevent him from forsaking the land in which he had been born, grown up and had worked all of his adult years, it had descended upon him with brutal fury, hammering and punishing him as only a wild, unchecked wind, gathering strength with each moment as it races across endless miles of barren flats, can do.

He could turn back, Dan reckoned, forget about Wyoming and J. J. Hamilton and taking on the job as foreman of the Double J ranch. He could stay right where he was—a cowhand on the Axhead—and avoid all this hell. Harvey Brazil, Axhead's owner, had the same as promised him the top-hand job when the present foreman—*caporal* folks called them down there low on the New Mexico-Texas border—retired, which would be in a couple of years.

He guessed it was old Percy Oliver who had made up Ragan's mind for him to cut loose from Brazil and accept the Wyoming offer. A man should never tie himself down young, grizzled, white-haired Percy had declared, but should move along, see as much of the country and do as much hell-raising as he could. Dan had finally accepted the oldster's advice: he'd sent word to Hamilton, telling the rancher he'd take the job and would be there by the prescribed day to take over—agreeing that if he failed to show up by that time it would indicate that he'd had a change of heart and Hamilton could go ahead and hand the Double J over to his second choice for foreman.

Hat pulled low, neckerchief tight over the lower half of his face, Ragan cracked his eyelids slightly and endeavored to make out where he presently was. On the broad, broken plains lying between New Mexico Territory and Texas, he knew, but that easily covered a hundred square miles.

He could determine no landmarks, no rising hills that should be somewhere to the west, nor see any lights that would indicate a town, or a ranch or homesteader. It was as if he were in a totally deserted world, a solitary being abandoned in a howling blizzard of stinging sand.

The day had started well enough. He had camped that night previous on the banks of the Canadian River, running full and fresh from the spring thaw in the high country, and gotten an early start while it was yet cool. But by noon the air had thickened and grown still and oppressive, and he realized long before he noted the darkening in the east that he was in for a sandstorm. There was nothing to do but continue along the trail and hope the wind, which could be savage enough on occasion to blind a man or tear clothing from his body, would alter course and bypass him.

It had been a useless hope. The ugly curtain rolling in from the east had spread, widening until it completely blocked the sky. The stillness increased, and there seemed to be no air left to breathe.

Then would have been the time to turn back, but Dan Ragan pressed doggedly on. The land ahead, he had noted, looked to be more broken, with low buttes and red-faced bluffs changing the monotonous flatness. Perhaps, once there, he could find protection of sorts for the sorrel he was riding and himself.

But the wind had come before he reached that possible haven. He had watched the snakeweed and the taller rabbitbush and white-flowered Apache Plume slowly stir into

4

life. The larks and the doves and other birds disappeared, and no living thing, not even the jackrabbits with their tall, black-tipped ears and tails, were to be seen.

It was around midafternoon that the wind, in full force, had struck. It had gathered its strength as it swept across the Panhandle, and by the time it had reached Dan Ragan and the hapless sorrel, it was moving at a furious, near irresistible pace and lashing everything in its path with merciless rage.

Ragan had soon altered course, quartering to the west rather than holding to a due north direction. By so doing he placed the sorrel's hindquarters to the wind and afforded himself some relief from the clumps of weeds, bits of wood, leaves and other debris, and the burning sand that it bore.

Such was only minimal protection, however. The sand and dust were a constant, whirling plague that enveloped them, imprisoning them no matter which way they might turn. The day had darkened and the heat had risen until the haze about them was almost suffocating. The sorrel began to labor although he was moving at no more than a slow walk. Several times Ragan had pulled to a halt, wet his bandanna, and swabbed the gelding's nostrils and lips and cleaned his eyes to relieve his suffering.

The storm should abate, Ragan felt. There was a saying down where he came from that the harder the wind blew, the sooner it would lay, but he was beginning to think there wasn't much truth to the old saw this early summer's day. An hour had passed since the wind had stuck, another and still a third, but still the burdened wind had lost none of its ferocity. By dark then, Ragan concluded, bringing to mind a different axiom. It would surely quit when night came. He was now discarding that belief; the dense pall of dust and sand moving westward only hastened the arrival of night.

Now, as he stood there in the swirling murk, rocked by the blasts, pelted by bits of trash, he finally admitted defeat and came to the inevitable conclusion. It was senseless to continue; he would have to halt and wait for daylight. The sorrel, skittish after the fall, punished by the wind, blinded and choked by dust and sand, could not be expected to go much farther.

Raising a hand, Dan cupped it over his partly open eyes in a futile attempt to shield them as he sought a better look at the country around him. There was nothing visible—only the sweeping clouds of gusting dust that engulfed him. He figured he should by then be in an area of short hills and arroyos glimpsed in the distance earlier before the storm had closed off his vision with its violence. And too, somewhere, were the buttes and bluffs he'd seen but had lost sight of.

A mutter of frustration slipped from Dan Ragan's sand-rimmed lips. Hell, there could be a Kansas barn ten feet away and he'd not see it! Turning, he stepped to the side of the sorrel, swung wearily up into the saddle, and raking the gelding with his spurs, started him forward again. Eventually he would find shelter of some kind—a deep wash, a bluff that faced the west and would thus get himself and his horse out of the howling wind, if not the dust and sand which filled the air. The latter would be a minor inconvenience, almost welcome, if it meant they had escaped the castigating wind.

The sorrel moved on slowly, hesitantly. Ragan could feel the animal trembling between his legs, and realized all the more that the sorrel was about done for and that he must soon halt and rest. Shortly he did pull to a stop, dismounted and again cleaned the gelding's nostrils and wiped his eyes with his damp bandanna, this time wetting the cloth afresh and squeezing a bit of the water into the gelding's mouth.

Back in the saddle, Dan once more looked about, desperately hoping to see something that would afford a measure of shelter. Again he failed. Shrugging resignedly, he put the sorrel into motion and moved off into the choking dimness. He'd look for another quarter hour, and if in that length of time he had not found a place, he'd give it up. He'd climb down, turn his back to the wind, and sit. The sorrel would instinctively face away from the blow and thus, together, they'd sweat out the storm.

Abruptly the gelding shied wildly. A coyote, head down, tail low, had bolted from beneath a clump of rabbitbush in which he had found shelter. The gaunt animal, eyes mere slits, quickly disappeared into the gloom.

The wind seemed to have slackened suddenly, although visibility was still confined to the area immediately surrounding him and the sorrel. Was the storm at last breaking up? Ragan concluded moments later, when the gelding was again proceeding slowly, that it was not. It was only that he had ridden into a lower area, probably a hollow or a deep wash, the east side of which was affording a degree of protection from the relentless gusts. How large the area was he could not determine, but it did not matter. He was now out of the wind's full force, and while it still howled and whistled and the air was laden with no less dust and sand, it was better. And it could be even better on ahead.

The arroyo, or swale, could become deeper, and there just might be trees—tough little cedars, perhaps, that were to be seen scattered about on the mesas, or maybe there'd even be a cottonwood or two. They liked water and often were found growing in the washes or along the edges.

Dan Ragan's thoughts broke off. He felt the sorrel go down under him again, and realized that the big horse, plodding blindly along, had gone over an embankment—either the edge of another arroyo or possibly a bluff; there was no time to speculate. Dan could do but one thing in that fragment of time—kick free of the stirrups as he'd done earlier, and launch himself from the saddle over the gelding's head.

2

Instinctively, Dan Ragan threw his arms forward to break his fall. He struck the ground hard, and came up solidly against an unyielding clump of brush. For several moments he lay motionless in the dust-filled gloom.

The sorrel . . . A shaft of fear shot through Dan as his thoughts centered on the horse. The gelding could have broken a leg —even his neck. Ragan rolled over and sat up. The big horse, on his feet, loomed over him. Ragan, forgetting his own pain, sprang upright. Reaching for the gelding's bridle, he caught it and steadied the trembling animal.

He could feel no blood on the gelding's legs, and with visibility so poor could see nothing either. But there was no comfort and assurance in that; the sorrel could have a broken bone and it still wouldn't show unless there was an open injury. Anxious, Ragan led the horse forward a few steps. Relief flooded through him. The gelding did not limp or favor any of his long legs.

Glancing about, Dan was able to determine that he was in an arroyo, and then reckoned he had been crossing a deep swale which he had mistaken for a wash. It had broken off abruptly into the arroyo, and such had caused the gelding's fall.

The wind was not striking them so forcefully in that lower area, and Ragan, worn as was his horse from bucking the frightful storm, wondered if he had not reached as good a place as he would find to wait out the blow.

Somewhere in the windy darkness beyond the arroyo Ragan heard a sound—a flat, slapping noise. He frowned and turned himself partly about to face the west. Rigid, struggling to block out the howling of the storm, he listened more intently. It could be a door, or perhaps a window shutter banging back and forth in the wind. Could there be a house, maybe a rancher's line shack, nearby?

There definitely was something, and taking up the sorrel's reins, Ragan moved off through the swirling black night toward the sound. As he crossed the somewhat narrow arroyo and started up a gentle slope, the wind again reached him and began to tear at him with its persistent force, whipping his jacket, striving to rip his hat, secured by a rawhide chin strap, from his head while it clouded his vision and choked his breathing with dust and sand.

But he pressed on, stumbling occasionally —once going to his knees when he stepped into a gopher or prairie dog's hole—all the while bearing toward the erratic slapping noise which seemingly had become more pronounced.

And then suddenly he reached the source —a low, slant-roofed shack. It was totally dark, appeared deserted, and the noise he had heard and followed was a door swinging wildly in the wind.

Ragan continued on, crossing the half-dozen strides to the shack, which regardless of condition would offer at least some protection from the ceaseless, maddening blow. Ignoring the flapping door, Dan led the sorrel around the side of the structure to the rear. A lean-to had been built off the end of the shack to provide shelter for two or three horses. The boards were rattling and creaking and sounded as if in danger of being torn loose and carried off into the turbulent night, but the lean-to was blocked by the shack itself from the driving wind and would provide good shelter for the weary sorrel. Ragan, leading the gelding in close to the forward wall, secured him to one of the posts.

Loosening the saddle cinch and slipping the bridle bit, he again cleared the horse's nostrils and eyes and gave him what water he could spare from his canteen. Then, taking his saddlebags and blanket roll, he retraced his steps to the front of the cabin. Reaching the doorway, one hand grasping and staying the swinging panel, Ragan endeavored to pierce the blackness within the creaking structure.

"Hello—inside!" he shouted above the noise of the storm.

There was no reply, and delaying no longer, Dan mounted the single step—a long plank laid crosswise in front of the entrance—and entered. Stepping immediately away from the drafty opening, he dropped his saddlebags and blanket roll to the floor, wheeled, and caught the door, now freed from his grip and again swinging back and forth. He discovered a wooden slide bolt as he felt around in the darkness, and pulling

13

the panel into closed position, he shot the bolt into place.

Immediately it was better inside the shack. The blasting wind no longer howled through the opening, and while the rattling and groaning of the walls and roof did not slacken, Dan no longer faced the sand and dust-laden wind.

He stood for a time in the center of the room, resting and relaxing, grateful to be out of the reach of the wild storm, and then, digging into a pocket for a match, thumb-nailed it into life. Holding it above his head, he glanced about. One room, a bunk built into a wall; shelves now empty but that once supported sacks and cans of foodstuff; a scorched place on the wood floor where a stove had stood, the hole in the ceiling above stuffed with rags.

The match burned its length, and Ragan, producing another, lit it and began to look about more closely. The cabin, probably once a line shack of some rancher's, apparently was being made use of now by drifters and other pilgrims. Because of such there might be a lamp or a lantern somewhere in the debris collected in the corners, Dan reasoned. A little light to break the smothering darkness would be more than welcome.

He found neither lamp nor lantern in his rummaging about, but he did turn up a candle, half used, and finding a shelf in a corner of the shack that escaped the gusty drafts entering through cracks in the walls, he lit it, dropped a bit of the tallow on the board to form a secure footing for the three-inch cylinder, and pressed it into position.

At once the gloom disappeared as the mellow glow of the small flame lit up the shack's neglected interior. Dan again paused, a tall, lean, angular man in his mid-twenties, with dark hair, light eyes, and the unmistakable stamp of a working cowhand on him, to listen to the shrieking wind beyond the cabin's thin walls.

They weren't much—only rough, unfinished boards no more than an inch thick and nailed to studs that were but little heavier—all of which protested noisily with each succeeding rush of the wind. The cracks between the boards had once been chinked with mud, but that had long since dried and fallen away to be replaced here and there with bits of rags and paper applied no doubt by some transient seeking comfort on a cold night, or perhaps a windy one such as this.

Ragan wheeled then, and picking up his saddlebags and blankets, crossed to the bunk. Just as well to sleep off the floor, he decided, but tired as he was, he found sleep far from him. Dropping the roll and the leather pouches on the slatted bunk, he turned again, and spurs clinking softly, he recrossed to the door. He'd have one more look at the sorrel, and get the canteen he'd forgotten to bring along, before bedding down for the night.

The wind wrenched the door from his hand when he slid back the bolt and began at once slamming it to and fro. Ragan made no effort to check the panel but circled around to the rear. The gelding was all right, standing hipshot and head down, out of the wind. Unhooking his canteen, Dan returned to the entrance of the cabin and, once more catching the door, stepped inside.

That candle's fragile flame had blown out instantly when the door had opened, and closing and bolting it behind him, Ragan produced another match and relit the wick. The room alight again, he crossed to the bunk, sat down, and pulling the canteen's cork, had himself a satisfying drink of water.

The winds blew in Wyoming, too, he'd been told, and he wondered if they did with as much force as those that swept across the Texas Panhandle and the eastern plains of

New Mexico—and if they carried as much dust and sand. If so, he thought wryly, he sure wasn't bettering himself insofar as weather was concerned.

The other Axhead cowhands had figured Ragan was looney to quit his job and head north. He was drawing top-hand wages on the biggest and best spread in that part of the country, and they just couldn't understand why he'd give that up.

Again, it was old Percy Oliver who had seen it differently.

"Man don't grow none staying put all his life—like I done," Oliver had said. "Now, if I had to do it all over again, I'd sure do mighty different! I'd not buckle down to one place, no, sir, I'd get on a good horse and do some riding. I'd make the big swing—from Mexico to Canada. And I'd have me a look at the old Mississip, then I'd head straight west like I was hunting the place where the sun goes down, only I'd be looking for the ocean. Yes, sir, I'd see it all, was I to get a chance to go around again!"

"Take a pile of money to do all that drifting," one of the hands sitting nearby had said.

"Hell, it don't take no big lot of money a'tall! A fellow can start out with a double eagle or two in his pants pocket, forking a good cayuse and toting a coffee pot and a little grub in his saddlebags and make out real good."

"On twenty—maybe forty—dollars?"

"Oh, I ain't saying that'd last him from hell to hallelujah, there being whiskey to buy now and then, and a lady to visit if he ain't lucky enough to find a right lonesome one. But a man shouldn't fret about running short of cash. He can always stop, find hisself a job and work for a spell—leastwise long enough to make a few dollars so's he can ride on.

"Now, boys, that's the important thing —ride on. It's mighty easy to find yourself a good job on a fine, big spread like Axhead where the grub's real good and the company's friendly and pleasing, but a man's got to put the temptation to rusticate behind him—just like the Lord told the devil. He's got to pass up that nice, inviting way of living and move on, else he's going to all of a sudden one day find hisself old and then it's too late to go."

"How's it happen you didn't follow your own advice, Percy?" another of the hired hands had asked. "Way I hear it, you been around Axhead since the year one!"

Oliver had grinned and scrubbed at his chin whiskers. "Seems dang nigh that long, sure enough! But answer is I didn't have the savvy then that I got now. If I had, I'd not be setting here now all full of misery and stiff as a poker—I'd be somewheres else enjoying myself—maybe setting on the bank of the Mississip fishing, or cooling myself off on one of them high country peaks in Colorado. Or maybe even I'd be up Oregon way tracking Indians for the government and. . . ."

Percy Oliver's voice trailed off as his chin sank lower in its bed of whiskers. Ragan had exchanged glances with the other hands and beckoned to one. Together they had lifted the frail oldster and placed him on his bunk where he began to snore peacefully as he fell into the slumber of the very old. Percy wouldn't like what they'd done, being a proud man, but he'd appreciate it just the same.

Dan had stuck to his decision to take the Wyoming job, not so much because he was harkening to Percy Oliver's words but, more to the point, because he hoped to better himself—and because of the fact that things on the Axhead were not good—a bit of confidential information given him by Harvey

Brazil, that moving on to work for J. J. Hamilton would be a big favor. Should things not work out, the rancher had assured him, he might again find a place for him on the payroll—but it was no promise.

Brazil need not worry, Dan thought as, eyes now heavy, he prepared to turn in. If things fell flat up in Wyoming, and he didn't like the looks of Montana and Canada, he'd—

Dan Ragan lunged to his feet, hand reaching for the pistol on his hip, as the door suddenly flung open. He had a fleeting glimpse of a man's strained, dust-streaked face and of his blood-stained shirt as he hung briefly in the opening before the wind snuffed out the candle and filled the shack with darkness.

"Help—help me!"

Dan heard the man's desperate cry above the screaming of the wind, and then came the sound of his falling to the floor.

3

Rigid, Dan Ragan rode out a long breath in
the blackness of the room while the raging
wind whistled and tore at him unchecked.
Then, hand flying away from the weapon on
his hip, he moved past the darker, huddled
shape on the floor and crossed to the cabin's
entrance. Seizing the flailing door, he pulled
it shut and secured it with the slide bolt.
Pivoting hurriedly, he stepped up to the shelf
where the candle had been placed, struck a
match to the tallow's wick, and as light
spread through the room, looked down at
the injured man.

Of average size, with dark hair, full
mustache, and several days' growth of
whiskers covering the lower half of his
strained face, he lay flat on his back. He was
dressed in usual range fashion—gray pants,

leather vest, checked shirt open at the neck, scarred boots, and a flat, plainsman-style hat held in place by a buckskin thong that passed over the crown and was tied under his chin.

A cartridge belt with most of the loops empty encircled his waist, and the butt of the pistol in his holster was standing upright, being partly trapped beneath his body. Nearby lay the saddlebags that he had been carrying across a shoulder—a handsome pair of Mexican, hand-tooled, black leather pouches that appeared to be well filled.

The man stirred weakly. Immediately Ragan knelt beside him and pulled aside the blood-and-dust-encrusted front of his shirt. He had been shot twice.

"Who . . . who the hell . . . are you?"

Ragan transferred his attention to the injured man's drawn features. His eyes had fluttered open and were filled with pain and anxiety—or fear.

"Dan Ragan. You got a name?"

The wounded man stirred. A frown pulled at his brow. "Hurley . . . Abner Hurley," he replied reservedly. "This your place?"

"No. Ducked in here getting out of the storm. You're in a mighty bad way. What happened?"

Hurley's wandering gaze drifted about the

room, came back to Dan. "Hard luck. You got a drink?"

Dan nodded, turned to the bunk and unbuckling one of his saddlebags, procured the bottle of whiskey he carried. He wasn't much of a drinker, but there were times, he'd found, when a swallow of liquor did a man a lot of good. Coming back around to Hurley, he held the bottle to the man's lips and poured a small quantity into his mouth.

Hurley gagged, swallowed, grinned weakly. "Obliged to you . . . Ragan. Was what I needed."

He relaxed, seemingly very weak. For several moments he lay still listening to the howling wind and then he brought his hard, overbright eyes to bear on Dan.

"Where you . . . headed?"

"Wyoming. Maybe Montana and Canada. You never said how you got shot up."

Hurley's glance lowered. His shoulders moved slightly. "Outlaws—damned, stinking outlaws. Been . . . running, hiding . . . from them. Lost myself . . . in that damn sandstorm. Heard . . . heard a door . . . banging. Made my way here."

"Where's your home?"

"Ain't knowing that." Hurley said, grimacing as pain shook him. "Got . . .

away from me. Fell off . . . my saddle. Been walking . . . ain't sure how . . . long. Hour or so . . . more seems like. You spare another . . . shot of that . . . redeye?"

Ragan placed the bottle again to Hurley's lips but the man, stronger now, took it into his own hand, and helped himself to a long drink.

"Plenty bad . . . out there," he said, returning the liquor to Dan. "Ain't meaning . . . the damned storm. Meaning the renegades . . . running loose. Country . . . country's lousy with . . . them."

Ragan agreed. It was common knowledge. Times were hard and men not necessarily outlaws were prowling the land doing any and all things to stay alive. "Bad all right," he said.

Hurley paused again as a spasm of pain wracked him, Then, settling back, "You working regular?"

Ragan said, "Yes. Quit the job I had yesterday. Riding north to take another. . . . Wish't there was something I could do for you, Hurley. I reckon you know you're shot up bad."

The corners of Abner Hurley's mouth pulled down. "I'm . . . I'm cashing in. Know that."

24

"Wasn't for the storm I maybe could get you to a doc. Must be a town somewheres close."

"There ain't." Hurley said wearily, "even if there was . . . ain't any use . . . you doing it. Can find a . . . couple of ranches up a . . . a ways. Nearest town's . . . Blackwater. It's three days . . . north . . . of here. Nope, just . . . talking to somebody . . . that's a mighty big . . . help. And that . . . that bottle of . . . your'n. Better'n any . . . damn doctor for me . . . shape I'm in."

Hurley's voice trailed off and he fell silent. Outside the wind continued to tear at the shack, rattling the loose boards, striving to rip the door and the shutter that covered the solitary window from their moorings. There was no let-up in its force, Ragan saw; instead its high, keening wail seemed even louder than earlier.

Pulling the blanket from his bunk, Ragan placed it under the dying man's head. Hurley, possibly, would be more comfortable on the slatted bunk, but getting him up onto it likely would cause the man more pain than the move would be worth.

"You from up here?" Dan asked, noting that Hurley had reopened his eyes.

Hurley stirred and groaned, grimacing

25

with pain. Something came loose from the shack outside, making a shrill squealing noise as it was whirled away by the wind.

"No . . . nope. Just been . . . through a couple . . . of times," Hurley replied. The words came out slowly and his voice dragged.

Ragan, curious, wondered about the wounds the man had sustained, but it was a question he could not ask. Hurley would tell him in his own good time, if he wished. A man didn't press another on matters such as that.

"You . . . you say you was . . . heading north?"

"Wyoming, mostly. Aim to—"

"You got a job . . . waiting for you?"

"Yeh—foreman's job. Double J ranch near a town called Laramie."

Hurley's mouth tightened. "Ain't . . . never been there. Heard . . . was fine . . . country."

"I'm hoping so. Ain't much for moving around, but a friend of mine—an old fellow—told me I ought to ride out, see everything I could. Said it was wrong to always stay put and—"

"He's right," Hurley said. "Man can't live this life . . . but once. He sure ought . . .

to . . . see everything he takes . . . a fancy to." He paused, brushed weakly at his mouth. "Reckon . . . I've done . . . my share. You spare me . . . another swallow . . . of your . . . whiskey?"

"Sure," Ragan said, and passed the bottle to him.

Hurley gripped the container with both hands, held it to his mouth, and swallowed deeply.

"Sure . . . sure am . . . obliged to you," he said, returning the bottle.

Ragan nodded. "There anything else I can do for you? I've got some water if you're wanting a drink, and I've got some jerky and biscuits in my saddlebags. Like to boil up some coffee but there's no stove in here and going outside, in that wind, it'd be—"

"Forget it," Hurley mumbled. "Be . . . a waste of your grub. Whiskey's best . . . for me where . . . I'm going. Sure obliged . . . to you. Reckon . . . I've done . . . said that."

Abner Hurley's skin had turned a sallow gray beneath its coating of dust and whiskers. His dark eyes, small to begin with, had receded deeper into their sockets and now appeared even smaller and had taken on the look of hard, round marbles.

"You . . . you figure . . . there ain't . . .

no chance of me . . . making it?'' he asked then as if to verify his own convictions.

Ragan shook his head. "Time like this a man's got to be honest. I don't figure you've got a chance. You lost a lot of blood and I expect those bullets are still in you. It's mighty hard for me to savvy how you've stayed alive this long."

"Was pure guts," Hurley muttered. "Most . . . of the time . . . I was traveling I . . . I plain didn't know where . . . I was or what . . . I was doing. First straight thinking . . . I've done . . . was after I . . . got here." He hesitated, listened to the moaning of the wind for a few moments, and then continued. "Was . . . was mighty lucky . . . finding you . . . here. Would've sure been . . . a bad thing . . . for me . . . if you hadn't."

Ragan's wide shoulders shifted. "Can't see that I've been much help. The whiskey—maybe—"

"You done . . . all you could. But . . . but that ain't what . . . what I'm thinking . . . about."

Ragan frowned. "Meaning?"

"Meaning I'm . . . I'm sure needing . . . a good friend. One I can . . . can figure on to . . . do me a favor."

"Sure do what I can for you, Hurley."

"That . . . that a promise?" the man said anxiously, struggling to pull himself upright. "That . . . that a for . . . for sure, honest . . . to God promise?"

Dan drew back slightly. "Sure—"

"You . . . you swear you'll . . . do what . . . I ask?"

"If I can," Ragan replied hesitantly. "I'm not much of a hand to buy a pig in a poke or do any promising before I know what—"

"Won't . . . won't be no . . . big chore," Hurley broke in. "And it'll . . . sure . . . keep me from . . . worrying—keep a . . . a dying man . . . from worrying."

Dan Ragan considered briefly, shrugged. "All right—you've got my promise. Tell me what you want done."

4

"Done . . . told you my . . . name so there—ain't no sense wasting . . . breath doing it . . . again," Hurley said, moving slightly on the dusty floor as if hoping to find more comfort. He frowned, seemingly searching for words, and then added: "I'm a rancher . . . leastwise . . . I was."

He paused, studying Dan Ragan in the weak light. "Maybe . . . maybe I don't . . . much look it, but when a man goes through . . . what I have . . . for the last couple . . . of days he ain't . . . likely to . . . to look so good."

Ragan shrugged. If his features had shown doubt, it was unintentional. "You said you were a rancher. I believe you."

"Was—ain't no . . . more," Hurley said slowly. "Don't matter . . . none. Sold out my . . . my place—lock, stock . . . and rain barrel. Been looking forward . . . to taking it . . . real easy . . . rest of my life—me and my wife . . . May."

Hurley stirred again, brushing wearily at his eyes. He had been a strong, muscular man, Dan realized, and that strength, now ebbing fast, was keeping him alive.

"Them—them saddlebags there," he continued after a time, pointing at the elaborately tooled leather pouches, "has . . . has got all my . . . money in them. Near thirty . . . thirty thousand . . . dollars. Gold . . . and greenbacks."

"Thirty thousand!" Ragan echoed, scrubbing at his jaw.

"I was . . . real careful—or thought I was. I reckon . . . now . . . I ought've got a bank . . . draft. But I wanted . . . to just once . . . carry a lot . . . of cash—my money. And I was wanting . . . wanting to walk in to . . . my wife . . . see the look . . . on her face when . . . when I handed it to her.

"Can see . . . now—I was . . . a damn fool thinking that . . . way—like some . . . wet-eared kid. But I done it and it's . . . sure too . . . late to bellyache . . . about it now."

"The money—it got something to do with

this favor you're wanting me to do?'' Ragan asked.

''Yeh—sure does. I'm getting . . . to it. Best . . . I tell you . . . the whole thing, howsomever, so's . . . so's you'll know . . . it all.''

Hurley paused once more. Speaking had become a greater effort for him and his words were less distinct than only minutes earlier.

''Ain't no need to hash it all over for me,'' Ragan said, wanting to spare the dying man as much as possible. ''Just tell me what you want done and I'll sure try and do it.''

Abner Hurley frowned. ''No—damn it! I . . . I want you . . . to know everything . . . in case you get . . . stopped. And anyway . . . May—my wife—she'll . . . want to know.''

Dan smiled. ''Suit yourself—''

The rancher reached for Ragan's bottle of whiskey, helped himself to a drink. Setting the container back on the floor, he lay quiet for a long minute as if gathering strength. Finally he settled his gaze on Ragan.

''All started a couple of days ago,'' he began, his voice much firmer. ''Ain't sure exact like . . . just when. Was down in Texas. Sold out my holdings—everything

—collected the money . . . and started . . . for home. Made sure nobody seen me when . . . when I rode out . . . and that nobody followed me.

"But I . . . I was wrong. Leastwise, I reckon they followed me . . . when I left town . . . because right after daylight—was this morning . . . I think—I seen four jaspers on . . . my trail and—"

A sudden gust of violent wind struck the shack with driving force, setting it to trembling and rattling. For a moment it appeared about to lift the cabin from its foundation and sweep it off into the wild night. Hurley did not stop talking and the words spoken during that brief span of time were lost to Dan in the surging noise.

"Tried shaking . . . them," the rancher was saying when his voice again became audible, "but couldn't. Pulled off . . . the trail then . . . hid in a grove of trees. That's when the shooting . . . started. They got me . . . first off—real good. Ain't for sure . . . I winged . . . one of them—but the shooting scared off . . . their horses. Was my chance. While they was out catching up . . . then, I made a run . . . for it . . . got away.

"Soon's I could I hauled up . . . doctored up the bullet . . . holes best . . . I could.

Stopped the bleeding . . . with some rags—
and then a while after that . . . the damn
wind got up . . . and next . . . next thing I
knowed . . . I was in the middle . . . of a hell
. . . of a sandstorm.''

"You lose the outlaws then?''

"Ain't sure. Seen them way back . . . top
of one of them little hills . . . about time the
storm hit. Know they seen me then . . . because they come on . . . fast. Don't think
they spotted me after . . . all that dust and
sand . . . got up. Man couldn't've . . . seen
something twenty feet . . . away much less
. . . a half mile. But they sort've had a . . .
line on me and could figure . . . where I'd be
. . . so for damn certain . . . they're still out
there . . . somewheres . . . hunting me. It
. . . it all right if I have another . . . shot of
your liquor?''

Hurley didn't wait for Ragan's approval;
he simply took up the bottle and had a
swallow. Again returning the whiskey to the
floor and once more falling silent, the man
closed his eyes. Dan considered him for a
long minute through the tan dust haze that
filled the room, and then shook his head
gently.

"This favor you're wanting done—maybe
you best tell me—''

"I'm coming to it," Hurley said, rousing. "Just having to . . . work up to it . . . so's you'll know. Now, like I said, I . . . I didn't see no more . . . of that bunch. Didn't see nobody . . . till I run into you . . . right here. But Peabody and them—"

"You know who the outlaws are?"

"Yeh—I know them—or leastwise, I've heard . . . of them," Hurley replied, correcting himself. "Best you get the . . . straight of this . . . in case you run up . . . against them. All mighty tough jaspers . . . hardcases. Don't try to shoot it out . . . with them. You wouldn't . . . have no chance a'tall.

"Peabody—his first name's Ed. Big man . . . riding a . . . gray horse. Another'n's Rufe Cobb. He's a skinny little bastard. Wears . . . wears one of them . . . fringed buckskin jackets and's riding . . . a black horse that's got white stockings. Man riding a bay'll be Arlie Redd. Last one's Dave Kitchens. He's real . . . mean and mighty . . . handy with his gun. Don't never . . . talk much—and he'd as soon . . . kill you as . . . swallow. He's redheaded and horse he's forking . . . is a black, too."

Ragan wiped at the dust clouding his eyes. He shook his head. "You sure must've got a good long look at them," he said. "And from plenty close."

"Why—why wouldn't I?" Hurley demanded in an angry voice. "Had me . . . pinned down for a whole . . . hour . . . maybe longer. Had plenty . . . of time to look them . . . over and figure out . . . who they was. Anyway, you for sure . . . keep a sharp eye out . . . for them. They'll still . . . be hunting for me."

"Not likely to take me for you—we don't look much alike," Dan said. "And I'm riding a sorrel. What was you on?"

"Bay . . . but don't you go . . . taking no chance. Just you stay . . . plenty clear of them . . . and ride fast as you . . . can to Blackwater."

"Blackwater? That where your wife's waiting?"

"Yeh. You'll find her . . . a house at the edge of town . . . east side. We ain't . . . been there long . . . so most folks won't . . . know us—her. She just sort of . . . moved in there . . . to wait . . . for me. I—I want . . . you to give . . . that money to her personally. She's a blonde woman . . . real pretty. You hand it to . . . her yourself. That clear?"

"Sure—"

"You . . . you do that . . . Ragan and I'll . . . give you a . . . thousand dollars. Reckon that's . . . mighty big pay . . . for doing a . . . piddling chore . . . like that, ain't it?"

Dan shook his head. "Keep your money. I won't charge a man for doing him a favor—'specially when it won't be none out of my way. I'm headed north, and I recollect you saying this town Blackwater is north of here."

Hurley was staring at Ragan. A deep frown knotted his forehead. "You're meaning that . . . ain't you? About . . . about not wanting . . . no pay?"

"That's what I said—"

"Yeh, you . . . for sure . . . did," Hurley agreed warily. "Now, you ain't figuring to . . . rook a dying man are you? Like maybe . . . keeping all . . . my money for yourself?"

Dan Ragan's features hardened. "Mister, if you're thinking I'd do something like that then the hell with it! I'll just get on my way, come morning if the wind's quit, and you can lay here till somebody else comes along to do it for you. I'm not in the habit of stealing from nobody—same as I've never gone back on my word to any man!"

Hurley lay quiet after Dan had finished,

his small, hard eyes fixed on the tall rider's face. Outside the wind seemed to have slackened somewhat, but it still rattled the old shack and set up wild noises as it tore at the roof and shrilled around the corners.

"I—I reckon . . . I knowed that, Ragan," Hurley said after a time, "and I'm asking your . . . pardon. I ain't seen too . . . many honest men . . . in my time but I know . . . I've met one now."

Dan made no comment, simply remaining motionless staring at the dwindling candle and listening to the wind. It seemed to be tapering off.

"You . . . you still willing to do me . . . the favor I'm asking?"

At the rancher's question, Ragan brought his attention back to the man. "Nothing's changed far as I'm concerned."

"Obliged. You got a mite riled . . . at what I said, and I . . . I was fearing you'd . . . changed your mind, maybe."

"Rubs me the wrong way for somebody to say I'm a crook or not take my word—"

"Was only . . . being careful," Hurley cut in. "You got to . . . understand—sort of see . . . things from my side. I'm handing over . . . a big pile of money . . . to a stranger . . . and asking him . . . to see that my wife gets

38

it. Only natural for me . . . to worry some . . . have doubts.''

Ragan gave that thought. "Yes, I reckon you've got a right . . . All you want me to do is carry the money to your wife—nothing else?"

Hurley nodded weakly, reaching out a limp hand. "You shake on it?"

Ragan took the rancher's cold fingers into his own. "Giving you my word."

Abner Hurley seemed to sink lower onto the floor as he settled back. "Good," he murmured, closing his eyes. "Sure . . . is a big load off'n . . . my mind, friend. Reckon I'll just . . . get myself . . . a bit of . . . shut-eye now."

Dan looked down at the man. It was a sleep that Hurley would not awaken from in this world, he realized.

"Yeh, we both better get some rest," he said, and then added softly: *"Adios."*

5

Dan Ragan had no idea of how long he slept —two, probably three hours. He had dozed off with the wind still tearing at the shack, rattling the boards with such force that it seemed certain to shake the frail structure into pieces, and awoke to find that a calm had settled over the land.

The candle had burned down to a flat pool in which lay the charred remnants of the wick, and immediately Dan crossed to the door and threw it open. It was first light and as the faint gray filled the dusty cabin, he turned and knelt beside Hurley.

The man was dead, as Ragan expected he would be. Rising, Dan stood looking down at the rancher, considering what he'd best do. The warning concerning the outlaw gang led by a man named Ed Peabody was still very much in the front of his mind and therefore governing his thoughts and action.

What must be done must be done quickly as well as carefully, he decided. If he was lucky enough to get away from the shack without being seen by the outlaws, his chances for fulfilling the promise he'd made Abner Hurley would be fairly good.

He must bear in mind, however—and it rankled him considerably—that he must avoid any confrontation with Peabody and his bunch. The odds would be four to one, and while in a shootout he was capable of doing more than just holding his own, the chances were that he'd come out a loser and that would put an end to the promise he'd made the dying rancher. He must stay alive to keep his word, and that meant running and hiding and avoiding a fight should he encounter the outlaws.

Shrugging off the distasteful thought, Ragan reached down, and unbuckling Hurley's gun belt, pulled it from around the man's body. Removing the pistol from its holster, and claiming the few brass shells from their loops, he laid the belt aside and thrust the weapon under his waistband. For what he could be getting himself into, he thought wryly, an extra gun might turn out to be a real comfort.

Hunching beside the dead man, Ragan removed the blanket he'd put under the rancher's head, and spreading it out on the floor, rolled Hurley onto it, wrapped it about him and secured it with the discarded cartridge belt. That done, he crossed to the door and hurried to where the sorrel was waiting.

The big gelding greeted him with an anxious whicker, and taking the small bag of oats he'd brought along for such moments, Ragan poured a quantity of the grain into the manger's box at the front of the lean-to, and then as the horse began to munch, Dan turned to searching about for a tool of some sort with which he could dig a grave.

He found nothing along the order of a spade or other conventional tool, and pressed by the urgent need to move out, to not tempt fate in favor of the outlaws by dallying too long at the cabin—which Peabody and his friends would certainly investigate once they spotted it—he settled for a board ripped from the shack and split to a fairly sharp point.

Hollowing out a shallow trench in a wash not far from the shack, Dan laid the rancher's blanket-shrouded body in it. With the soil he'd removed from the trench, as well as caving in the sides of the gully to cover the body, he managed a suitable grave and one that would be safe from wild animals. By the time he was finished the sky to the east was shot with early morning color.

Ragan paused for a minute to stare off into the distance while he rested his muscles, unaccustomed to such labor. Turning to the gelding, snuffling hopefully about in the manger for any grain he might have missed, Dan tightened his saddle and slipped the bridle into place. Jerking the tie rope loose, he then led the horse around to the front of the shack.

He could use a bit of breakfast—at least a cup of coffee—but he had a deep-set feeling that he didn't have the time, that he'd best put it off until he was well away from the cabin. Stepping hurriedly into the structure, he collected his belongings, and hanging the black saddlebags over a shoulder, returned to the gelding. Mounting quickly, he rode off, heading north on the trail.

There was little evidence of the windstorm's passing. The shrubs, mostly Apache Plume, rabbitbush and oak brush, grew close to the ground and possessed a tough flexibility; offering little resistance to the wind, they had sustained no damage. Nor did the round clumps of snakeweed or stalks of tassle grass. Only where there had been a solid obstruction to the wind such as a rock ledge or similar formation were there signs —and that in the form of drifted sand.

Ragan rode steadily for the first hour, halting finally beside a lone cedar on the summit of a rise to have a look back over the country he had just traveled.

He came to immediate attention. Two riders were on the trail and coming on fast. They could only have passed by the shack and most likely had seen him when he rode off from it—or suspected he had been there.

But Hurley had said there were four in the outlaw gang that was trailing him. These, probably, were just two pilgrims on their way north. Dan gave that consideration for a brief time while the sorrel rested, and then, only partly convinced by his reasoning, rode on.

The sight of how fast the pair had been moving persistently plagued Dan Ragan's mind and shortly, when he reached a wide arroyo along which mesquite and other wild growth formed a dense border, he turned from the trail and struck a due west course. He'd let the riders get by, thus putting them

44

out in front of him. Under the circumstances he'd feel much better with them there rather than at his back.

Dan reached the opposite side of the big, sandy-floored wash, a four-foot-high wall stabilized with embedded rocks and growing weeds, and drew to a halt. He'd wait there for an hour or so, allow the riders to pass, and then resume the trail. Meanwhile he'd have himself a little something to eat. Coffee—as much as he wanted and needed a cup, he would still have to wait; smoke, even from a fire made with dead and completely dry wood, might be seen. It was best he hold off until he was certain the two riders were well out in front of him and there were no others to be seen.

Swinging down from the saddle, Ragan took the sack of jerky from his saddlebags and selected several pieces. Adding to them a couple of the biscuits he had included in his supply of trail grub, he found a place on the bank of the wash and sat down to eat. Nearby the sorrel nuzzled about in the weeds and short grass that grew along the edge of the arroyo's bed.

The sun was now well on its way, and the cloud-free sky could only be a promise of heat. It would be a pleasing change from the fierce dust and sandstorm of the preceding day, Ragan thought, but a rain would be the most welcome.

The minutes dragged by. Finished with his meal, one washed down with water from his canteen, Ragan stirred restlessly. He should be on his way. He had departed Brazil's Axhead ranch in ample time to reach Wyoming and claim the job being held for him—until the first of the month—if he proceeded at a normal pace. He was unwilling to press his luck and fall behind schedule to any extent. He would be passing through strange country where he had no idea of what conditions would be, and he could get delayed. He had allowed for such, but only up to a point.

Nevertheless, despite his need to move on, Ragan waited out for what he judged was a full hour—plenty of time for the riders to draw abreast, pass by, and get well ahead.

Still in the wash, with the sorrel walking quietly on the soft sand, and yet a dozen yards from where it ended and the well marked course to the north lay, Ragan drew his horse to a quick stop. The strong smell of tobacco smoke hit him, and then a moment later he caught the sound of voices.

"He's got to be along here somewheres," one said.

"For sure," another agreed. "That bastard couldn't've got by me and Rufe without us seeing him."

6

The outlaws. Ragan's jaw tightened and tension began to build within him. How had Peabody and his friends Kitchens, Cobb, and Redd managed to get ahead of him?

There could be but one explanation. In trailing Hurley they had bypassed the cabin and continued north along the trail. Eventually, deciding the rancher was not in front of them and that they had overshot him during the storm, they had split up—two doubling back while the remaining pair had stayed where they were and set up a sort of ambush. The riders he had seen earlier were the two who had doubled back.

"That jasper you was following—you for damn sure he was Hurley?"

It was the same voice—deep, rasping, and sharp with angry impatience.

"Told you what I figured, Ed," the reply came. "Was too far off to get a good, square look at his face, even with my glass. Anyway, had his back to me all the time— but it was Hurley, all right. I spotted them fancy Mex saddlebags. Arlie seen them, too—through my glass."

"Has to be him, all right," the angry voice, evidently Ed Peabody, replied. "But where the hell'd he go? Got to be somewhere close."

"Maybe he spotted us and cut off the trail and's headed cross country—"

"For where?" Peabody demanded. "Ain't nothing but flats both ways—and there ain't no town for a hundred miles either direction. And there's no water."

"Reckon you're right. He ain't that big a damn fool."

"Well, we know pretty much he'll just keep going north," a different voice said. "Thing for us to do is mount up and head that way, too. Sooner or later we're bound to spot him again."

Dan waited no longer. Cutting the sorrel slowly about, he walked the big horse quietly back across the wash until he reached its yonder side, and then, once up on the brushy flat that lay to the west, broke the gelding

49

into a fast lope.

He had no choice but to continue on a northerly course. Wyoming and his job lay in that direction, and he could afford no lengthy detours to other points. Also, the town of Blackwater where May Hurley lived and where he would rid himself of the money he was carrying, was to the north.

Ragan maintained a good pace, not pressing the sorrel but holding him steady for the first hour—all the while keeping well clear of the trail which he could see now and then through the brush that lined the arroyo. Evidently the big wash was one of the major drains of the mountains that rose blue-gray against the sky, far to the northwest, and undoubtedly ran bank-full on the occasions when heavy rainstorms visited the area.

When dark patches of sweat began to appear on the sorrel's hide, Dan slowed the horse to a walk, and finally, in the filigree shade of a mesquite, halted. The gelding was beginning to show his need for water—running low in the canteen—and Ragan, following earlier procedure, soaked his bandanna, wiped the horse's lips, and squeezed the cloth dry into his mouth.

There should be water somewhere along the trail, Dan was certain. Such routes could be depended upon to follow a course that would, somewhere along the way, pass a spring or a creek. Such was more or less a rule, and this one, a main, well-used road that wound its way through the low hills and arroyos, past the red-faced bluffs and across the flats to Colorado, Kansas, and points farther on, would be no exception.

But as morning grew old and the sun became increasingly hotter with no sign of stream or a spring anywhere, Ragan began to wonder and to have doubts. Noon came, and with it the short hills through which he had been passing faded, and he found himself on a vast plateau. But the arroyo, now much narrower and deeper, was still in evidence.

Dan got his next glimpse of the outlaws at that time. They were on the trail—four indistinct figures—a good two miles in the distance. They would not have seen him, he believed. Being off the trail on a paralleling course, and keeping to the low-lying country and behind the brush as much as possible, he would not have been visible to them. But now he had reached an area where that advantage would be lost to him as the plain, stretching out before him, appeared to offer little in the way of cover.

Studying it through eyes narrowed to cut

down the glare, Ragan swore impatiently. Why the hell had he let himself in for this? If he had refused Hurley's plea to deliver the money to his wife—just turned the man down flat—he'd be out there now on the trail, heading straight for the next town and having no worries whatsoever.

But how could he, in all good conscience, turn down a dying man's request—especially when it was plain the man had gone through hell in his efforts to reach his home and wife and preserve their lifetime earnings?

Dan shrugged. There was little gained in hashing over the decision he'd made to help Hurley now. What he had done was done, and he'd live with it. Glancing again to the distant outlaws, he raked the sorrel with his spurs and moved on.

He began to angle west slightly, following a low ridge on the plain that afforded some protection from being seen by anyone on the trail. Keeping the sorrel again to a steady pace, he rode on through the noon heat, hoping to eventually come to water and that he would be far enough away from Peabody and the other outlaws to satisfy the needs of the sorrel and himself before they could spot him and close in.

Late in the afternoon Ragan found himself

back near the trail—and less than a mile from the outlaws. The rise he had followed had formed an arc, and during the process of traveling along its curve as he sought to remain out of sight, the trail had maintained a straight line which allowed Peabody and his friends to draw much closer.

They were not long in spotting him. He had no sooner seen them than they, in turn, caught sight of him. Dan saw them pause briefly, and then abruptly all four men wheeled, broke their horses into a gallop and at once began to narrow the distance that separated him from them.

Ragan glanced about. There appeared to be heavier brush to the west. Immediately he swung the sorrel around and started, on a right angle course from the trail, for the band of dense growth. If he could get himself far enough to the side, there was a good chance he could remove himself from the outlaws' view, thanks to a low rise in the plain. He could then decide what was best to do—continue on and resume his northerly course, double back for a few miles, or simply find a place to hide and lie low until the outlaws gave it up.

The sorrel covered a quarter mile of hard-surfaced ground at good speed, and then as they dropped off into a narrow wash floored with loose sand, he began to slow and tire. Dan, aware that Peabody and the others could no longer see him but could only guess at the direction he had taken, eased up on the gelding.

And then well on to the northwest, beyond the strip of brush, he saw the darker blur of trees—a small grove, it appeared to him. A hard grin cracked his lips as he wiped at the sweat misting his eyes. It could only mean a spring. If he followed out the arroyo they were in, it likely would lead him to the grove while permitting him to stay below the level of the plain and not visible to the outlaws. Maybe he was going to get lucky after all— he'd just about concluded his luck had run out.

Urging the sorrel on, and keeping an eye in the direction of the trail, Ragan pointed for the grove. The arroyo proved to be a disappointment, however, when it began to curve toward some distant hills. Forsaking it—and once again on the plateau—he continued to bear for the trees. Fortunately the roll in the plain kept him hidden from the trail, and since there were no signs now of the outlaws following, he reckoned he had again given them the slip. It was not a particularly comforting thought, however; chances were they would end up once more in front of him, and if they became aware of the fact—which they surely would after a time—they had but to wait and permit him to ride into their ambush.

In the diamond-clear atmosphere of the high-country mesa, the grove had seemed but a few miles distant—a place to be reached within an hour at most. It was near sundown, however, when Dan approached the first of the trees and saw the glint of water within them.

Sighing with relief, he glanced back a final time to assure himself there were no signs of the outlaws, and seeing nothing silhouetted against the darkening skyline, urged the sorrel on.

Almost immediately he brought the gelding to a halt. Close by, somewhere in the grove ahead, a flurry of gunshots had broken out.

7

Ragan sat quietly in his saddle, straining to hear sounds that would indicate what was taking place in the depths of the grove. The gunshots—four in all—could mean anything: a pilgrim making camp for the night and shooting a rabbit or other game for the evening meal, or even someone killing a rattlesnake.

But it could also indicate trouble, and for that reason, if he intended to ride on in, he should do so carefully. Dan experienced a few moments of indecision; he needed water for himself as well as his horse, and he needed to eat. On the other hand he felt he could afford no lengthy delay, and that was just what he could involve himself in if he encountered someone in serious difficulty.

The uncertainty lasted but a brief time. No

decent man turned his back on a fellow being at a time of trouble on the trail; he did what he could to help regardless of personal inconvenience.

Glancing back again over his shoulder—Peabody and his gang might also have heard the gunshots—and finding the mesa still devoid of riders, Dan started the sorrel toward the grove, pointing for a finger of trees and brush that jutted out from the main body of the oasislike area. Reaching that, he rode into the shadowy aisles among the cottonwoods and other growth, and halted.

There had been no more gunshots and he had detected no other sounds, but now the smell of a campfire, borne on the light breeze, came to him. He might have guessed right, he reckoned. The shooting likely had been a traveler killing a varmint of some sort, but a natural wariness refused to let Dan accept the explanation at face value; it was only prudent to find out for certain.

Walking the sorrel slowly, he moved forward through the trees, shielded fairly well now not only by the trunks of the sycamores and cottonwoods but by the deep shadows the setting sun was casting among them.

Shortly he heard the rumble of voices. The

odor of smoke grew stronger. He'd best proceed now on foot, Ragan decided, and pulling to a stop, he dismounted, tied the gelding to a sapling, and, drawing his gun, continued.

He saw the wagon first—an ordinary farm vehicle with an arching, white canvas top, in which two cross seats had been built for passengers. Then he saw the dead men.

Instantly Dan ducked in behind the screen of brush that fringed a clearing while a grimness settled over him. Two men, both elderly, lay just beyond the wagon. Both had been shot. Near the front of the vehicle were four women—all fairly young. Their hands had been bound behind their backs, and to prevent them from escaping, each was also tied to the wagon's tongue.

In the center of the camp six men, bearded, dressed in worn, stained clothing, were squatting near the fire hungrily eating from a large kettle into which they were dipping chunks of bread, totally ignoring the plates, spoons, forks, and other conveniences placed nearby.

It was not difficult to see what had happened. The pilgrims, two men and the four young women, had halted at the spring in the grove to make camp for the night. The

58

men—lawless renegades from all appearances —had come upon them, or possibly had been waiting in the grove for just such an opportunity. They had jumped the pilgrims, shot the two men, and after making certain the women would not get away, fell to satisfying their hunger. Once they had finished the meal, they undoubtedly planned to turn their attention to the helpless prisoners.

It was no time for gentlemanly heroics, nor for following the rules of fair play. If he failed to drive off the renegades and himself fell victim to their guns, the women would be in for a night of horror. It did not occur to Dan Ragan at that moment to simply back off and ride on, looking to his own best interests and welfare. Nor did he allow himself to be deterred by the fact that he was outnumbered and outgunned—six to one —by ruthless men who thought nothing of killing; his consideration centered only on how best to cope with the situation.

He had two pistols, his own and the one he'd taken from Abner Hurley's body. That helped some, although, as he'd noted earlier, the rancher's weapon was of a different caliber—a forty-four, while he carried a forty-five. But it was fully loaded and he could make good use of it.

"Where we going from here?"

One of the outlaws had finished eating. He had risen, and was staring at the women. A reply came from the others, each with his own idea of a future destination, but the words were low and therefore inaudible to Ragan just as it had been when he first saw them from the brush.

He must act now, catch the renegades while they were occupied and take advantage of the slight edge that gave him. If he waited much longer all would have satisfied their hunger and his job would be more difficult.

Abruptly Ragan came to his feet. With Hurley's forty-four in his right hand, he stepped out of the brush into the clearing. Instantly a yell went up from one of the outlaws hunkered near the fire.

The man who had finished his meal earlier whirled, weapon out. Ragan dropped him before he could trigger his pistol, and drove another bullet into a second renegade lunging upright. Two others of the party, rocking to one side, opened up with their guns and Dan heard the clip of bullets cutting through the brush behind him.

Instantly he began to move, weaving and dodging from side to side, all the while thumbing the hammer of the weapon he was holding and firing steadily at the renegades, now vague figures in the failing light and drifting gunsmoke and dust.

Another of the outlaws went down, falling across the fire and sending up a shower of sparks. Through the hammering of the guns Dan could hear one of the women screaming.

The forty-four clicked on an empty cartridge. Dan thrust the useless weapon under his belt, and, still moving, drew his own gun and continued firing. But his targets were now hurrying away. Through the haze he saw the remaining three men running toward the far side of the clearing, and, moving farther to his right, saw the horses tethered there.

Taking quick aim at the fleeing renegades, he pressed off the trigger of his weapon. The hammer came down on a spent shell, as had the forty-four a few moments earlier. Cursing, Ragan stepped back into the brush, and rodding out the empties from the weapon's cylinder, hastily reloaded and returned to the clearing.

He was too late. The outlaws had mounted and ridden off. Dan remained motionless there in the closing night, listening for sounds of the renegades' flight. It could be they had merely left the camp and were planning to circle back as soon as they got themselves organized. He thought he could hear the drumming of fast-running horses, but could not be sure. He could only hope that it was the outlaws leaving the grove.

Pivoting, Ragan dropped back to where he had left the sorrel, and freeing it, he mounted and rode quickly into camp. Drawing up beside the three downed outlaws, he dropped from the saddle and gave each a hurried examination. There was nothing to fear from any of them.

Ragan crossed to the women as the sorrel moved off on his own toward the spring to water. Drawing his knife he began to slash their bonds.

"We've got to get away from here—fast!" he said in a tight, harsh voice.

8

Immediately, as Ragan cut the bonds of the young women, each hurried to where the two men lay. One, the eldest of the four apparently, dropped to her knees beside the still bodies, and grasping the arm of one, rolled him onto his back.

"Dead," she murmured, glancing up at the others gathered about her. "Pa's dead."

She moved a bit forward to the man lying just beyond her parent. Turning him face up also, she made a brief examination.

"So's Uncle Ben," she said, coming to her feet.

Features set, she put her attention on the remaining girls. That they were sisters was self-evident. Even in the dim light Dan could see the strong family resemblance. Silent, he watched them gather into a close circle, holding and comforting each other as they sought to weather the shock. They had been to hell and back in those past minutes, and despite the urgent need to move on, to get away from the clearing where they were easy targets for the renegades, he felt he could not disturb them in their moment of loss.

He wondered again if Peabody and his outlaw friends had heard the gunshots. The clearing was not near the trail, but sound carried for a great distance in the high country and there was a distinct possibility that they had. Abruptly Dan moved over to where the women were standing. "I'm sorry, ladies—but it's not safe to hang around here any longer."

The taller and older woman disengaged herself and turned to him. She had blue eyes that looked almost black in the poor light and her dark hair, having come loose probably when she was tied up, now hung about her neck and shoulders in thick folds. There was an air of authority—almost of impatience—to her, and it was evident the others looked to her for direction.

"I'm Cameo Wakefield," she said in a strong voice. "My sisters and I are grateful to you for—"

"Best you save that till later," Ragan

cut in, glancing about. "Three of that bunch got away—and they could be coming back. Probably will, soon as they realize there's only one of me. Want you to get on your horses—can use two of those the outlaws were riding—and follow me."

Cameo Wakefield shook her head. "No, we're not leaving Pa and Uncle Ben here. Besides, those saddle tramps won't take us by surprise again."

"Maybe," Dan said, frowning. Then, "All right, let's get your team hitched up. I'll load the bodies in the wagon."

Cameo nodded briskly, then turned her attention to the sister standing to her left. Unlike the older woman, she was a blonde and had a calm sweetness to her features.

"Angie, you collect the bedding," she said, and added to the one next to her, dark and pretty and evidently the youngest of all, "Lila, you gather up the cooking utensils, and the food and whatever else is laying around that's ours and put it in the wagon. Pearl, you best help me with the team."

Pearl, another blonde, smiled tightly and hurried off toward the horses standing in the trees at the edge of the grove. Ragan, relieved at the immediacy of the Wakefield girls' attitude and actions, crossed to the rear of the canvas-topped vehicle, and, lifting the metal checks, allowed the tailgate to open and swing down. Turning, he then moved to where the Wakefield men lay. Cameo was there ahead of him and as he approached she raised her eyes to him.

"Pa and Uncle Ben tried to fight them off—but they never had a chance. I—I think they knew that."

"Hardcase bunch for certain," Dan agreed. "How'd it happen they caught you not looking? Don't you know the country's plain overrun with trash like them?"

Cameo shook her head, shifting her gaze to where Pearl was leading the team up to the wagon's tongue. "I guess we never thought about it. We'd just sat down to eat when they came riding into our camp— yelling and shooting. Uncle Ben was hit right off—right at the start—Pa a bit later."

Ragan swept the fringe of the clearing with sharp eyes. It was almost full dark, and if the renegades were back and hiding in the brush, it would be impossible to see them. Bending down, he picked up Wakefield, a slight, lean man who was no burden at all, and carried him to the wagon. Placing him on the floor under the extra seats that had been installed, he returned quickly to the second man and brought him to the vehicle also. Laying him alongside Wakefield—his brother, apparently—Dan took a blanket that was draped across the rear seat and covered the bodies with it.

Lila, the pale oval of her youthful face sober in the darkness, was standing behind him when he finished. She was holding several pots and dishes. Ragan took them from her. The girl wheeled wordlessly as he set them in the wagonbed, and retraced her steps to the fire for a second load. At that moment Cameo came up carrying the gun-belts and weapons she'd stripped from the dead outlaws.

"These might come in handy," she said, dropping them onto one of the seats, continuing on toward the front of the wagon to assist her sister Pearl.

Again probing the brush and once more failing to see any sign of the renegades, Dan headed back across the clearing to get his own horse. He found the sorrel grazing on the grass near the spring. Taking a minute to refill his canteen, Ragan swung aboard the big horse and returned to the Wakefield wagon.

The team was in harness and ready to move out. The last of the family belongings were aboard. As he rode up, urgency pressing him hard, Lila and Angie quickly climbed into the vehicle and assumed the center of the two extra seats. Cameo and the sister she had addressed as Pearl already occupied the driver's seat. Taking up the reins, the older woman nodded to him.

"Lead the way. Road's over to the right a bit if you're looking for it."

Ragan swung in beside the team, a pair of bays that looked to be in need of rest, and paused. They should head in the direction the family was going—probably to their ranch or homestead. He had second thoughts on the matter. The important thing was to get away from the spring and the clearing —and be as far away as possible in the event the renegades returned—or Peabody and his crowd showed up. They could move for an hour, then halt. At that time he could find out where the Wakefields lived and decide what to do about it.

"Expect it'll be smarter if we stay clear of the road," Dan said. Moving out in front of the bay team, he struck off through the trees.

He had again become involved in a problem that was going to cost him time unless he was careful, Ragan cautioned himself. And he had already committed himself to doing a favor that likely would delay him several days before he was done with it. Bearing that in mind, it was clear he could hardly afford to spare much time to the Wakefields—and he hoped he would not be called upon to do so. If they lived somewhere near—and in the right direction —all well and good. Otherwise . . .

Dan let his thoughts trickle off, putting his mind to the chore of getting the team and wagon through the grove. Night had closed in and there was now only the light of the stars and moon filtering down through the branches of the trees to aid him in choosing a way.

It was slow and tedious, and several times he led them into dead ends he at first figured to be clear aisles, and on each occasion Cameo expertly backed the vehicle out. That the eldest Wakefield sister was a good hand with horses was quickly apparent, and as such she stirred up considerable admiration in Ragan.

At such incidents it was the loss of time that troubled Dan. They were moving all too slowly, but there was no help for it. Admittedly, taking the established road would have made for faster traveling, but it also could lead them into an ambush, should it be that the renegades, electing not to return to the clearing and face him, were waiting somewhere along its narrow length.

Frowning, he drew in the sorrel and allowed the wagon to pull up beside him. He nodded to Cameo, vaguely visible in the shadowy night.

"You know this grove? We anywhere near the end of it?"

"It can't be more than a quarter mile to the edge—near as I can remember," she replied.

"Then what?"

"Low hills—brush. No trees."

Ragan swore softly. Open country, or pretty much so. A wagon would be in view for a considerable distance.

"How much farther do you think we'll have to go before it's safe to stop?" Cameo asked then, leaning forward, elbows on her knees as she gripped the lines. "We've had a long day—a hard one. And I doubt the horses can go much farther."

Ragan cast a critical eye at the team. Even in the darkness it was easy to see that they were laboring, but to halt and allow them to rest would be dangerous. Dan shrugged as he considered that thought. It would be just as dangerous that coming day when they reached open country and the horses were in no condition to make a run for it should the renegades spot them and attack.

"You think those—those outlaws are still hanging around?" Pearl asked.

"Of course he does!" Cameo replied snappishly. "That's why we're in such a hurry."

"I'm pretty sure they're around some-where close," Dan said when Cameo had finished. "But we'll have to chance it and pull in for the rest of the night. If luck's with us, they'll lay low till sunup when they can see what they're doing—and we'll want your horses in good shape for a hard run if they spot us."

Dan hesitated, listening to the far off moaning of a dove for a moment. Then: "When we get to the edge of the grove we'll stop and camp, wait for daylight."

9

They halted in a shallow swale not far from the end of the grove. Brush was plentiful and Ragan believed they would be as safe there from search as they would be anywhere in the area. If the three survivors of the renegade gang took it in mind to hunt them down, he doubted there was any place among the trees where he and the Wakefield women could effectively hide a canvas-topped wagon from view.

As he rode the sorrel off to one side of the small, grassy clearing to dismount and tie the animal to a convenient tree, Angie came up and stood beside him. When he had completed his chore, he wheeled and faced her questioningly.

"Cameo wants to know if we should un-hitch the horses and bring them over here, or

72

leave them stand in their harness?" she asked, smiling.

Ragan shrugged. He could have spent a good part of that night traveling north but instead was being forced to bed down and play nursemaid to four women—and that fact had turned him impatient.

"Bring them over here," he replied shortly, and added, "If that bunch takes after us in the morning we'll never be able to outrun them, anyway."

Angie nodded, smiled again, and hurried away. Dan, leaving the sorrel saddled and bridled for later use, glanced about in the shadow filled darkness until he located a fair sized tree. Making his way to it, he climbed to the first limb. Settling himself, he began a slow search of the grove, looking for the glare of a campfire and listening for sounds.

He could see nothing, and there were only the usual muted noises made by birds and animals. He knew they were too far from the road to hear horses moving on it. Dan had thought he might pick up the sound of the renegades if they were working through the grove, but there was no indication of such; the men, he hoped again, had also made camp somewhere and were awaiting daylight.

When he returned to the coulee, the

Wakefield girls had taken the pots and pans from the wagon and made preparations for a meal.

"There won't be any coffee," Cameo announced as he glanced to where the horses stood—picketed well apart so that each would have ample grazing. "I didn't think a fire would be a good idea."

"It wouldn't," Ragan said, peering through the half dark at the food placed on a makeshift table—one probably built by the girl's father or uncle for just such occasions. In the pale light shed by the moon and stars he could see that it was crude but sturdy.

"There's plenty of fried rabbit and quail. And there's potatoes and corn—and biscuits," Pearl said. "It's all cold, of course."

"And for dessert there's apple pie and honey," Cameo finished.

"Sounds mighty good," Ragan said, his mood and manner softening. He hadn't eaten, it seemed to him, for days, and he had built up a towering hunger.

Pearl, taking one of the plates, heaped it with meat and vegetables and several biscuits and handed it to him. Completing the serving with a fork, she nodded, and stepping back, joined her sisters gathered at the front of the wagon.

The night was warm, and the light from the moon as it climbed higher into the dark, velvet canopy of the sky, had become brighter, transforming the swale into a softly illumined bowl. From nearby an owl hooted forlornly and off somewhere in the grove a dog barked—one that had probably strayed from a passing party of travelers and taken up residence among the trees.

"We've been talking about Pa and Uncle Ben," Cameo said, separating from the others and coming over to where he squatted on his heels. "We don't know whether to bury them here in the grove or take them on to the ranch."

Ragan gave the matter thought. The weather was much too hot to delay the burial for long. "How much farther to your place?"

"One day—if we move fast."

Dan's shoulders stirred. "Expect you can wait until you get there, if it's no farther away than that."

Cameo nodded. "That's what I told Pearl and the other girls—and I'd like it that way. Pa and Uncle Ben ought to be buried on the ranch they worked so hard to build up. We'll wait."

Ragan had resumed his meal, vaguely

aware now of the steady attention all four Wakefield women were paying him. Brushing it off as pure curiosity, he voiced the question that could mean much to him.

"Which way to your ranch?"

"It's called the Circle W—and it's west and a bit south of here."

Ragan swore silently as he chewed on a piece of rabbit. Getting the Wakefield women safely home would mean swinging off course and losing two, perhaps three days—if they didn't run into more trouble! His mouth tightened into a hard, straight line. It was beginning to look as if he wasn't intended to take that job in Wyoming!

Cameo, sensing a problem on his part, considered him closely in the pale light. "Which way were you going when you ran into us?"

Dan finished off the last of the fried potatoes, rose, and set his empty plate on the table. "North to Wyoming. Got a job waiting for me there," he answered.

"Then looking out for us is out of your way—"

Ragan smiled faintly. "Reckon I'll manage. You coming from somewhere special or were you all just Sunday socializing back there at the spring?"

"Hardly that," Cameo said a bit stiffly. "We were returning from a wedding—our sister Patience. It was held over in Red Bluff—that's a town in the Staked Plains country."

Ragan nodded, pulled out his sack of tobacco and packet of brown papers and began to roll a cigarette. "I've been there."

"We went all that way and back with no trouble until we got to here—only a day away from home."

"That's the way luck works sometimes," Dan said. "There any more family at your ranch—a brother or two, maybe?"

"No, there's just the four of us girls now, and three or four hired hands." Cameo hesitated, giving her sisters a thoughtful look. "It's going to be up to us to run the place now." Abruptly she frowned, then smiled. "We never did get around to introducing ourselves—properly, I mean. We told you some names, nothing more. I'm Cameo."

Ragan exhaled a cloud of smoke, inclined his head slightly. "I remember. I'm Dan Ragan."

"All right, Dan—if you don't mind me calling you by your first name."

"Sure—why not?"

"Then you call me Cameo. Now, I'll try to clear up my sisters for you. The youngest one there, the one with the dark hair is Delilah. We call her Lila for short. Pearl is the one wearing the yellow shirtwaist. The tall one with the scarf on her head is Angie. She looks just like Ma—did."

"Did? I wondered where—why—"

"Ma died two years ago. We had a real bad winter and she caught lung fever." Cameo half turned, facing her sisters across the narrow strip of moon and starlit ground. "Girls, our friend here is Dan Ragan. I've told him who each of you is."

The Wakefield sisters all smiled, nodded. Angie said: "We'll never be able to thank you for all you've done for us. When I think what would have happened if you hadn't come along and—"

The woman's voice broke and she looked down. Pearl moved in closer, placed an arm about her shoulders.

"But he did come along, Angie. That's the important thing. God has a way of taking care of those who need help."

A silence fell over the clearing after that, broken only by the hushed sounds of the night and the restless shifting of the tired horses.

"Are you going to stay with us all the way to the ranch, Mr. Ragan?" It was Lila who broke the quiet with her question.

"Dan," he said, correcting her and gaining a few moments to think—and decide. "I—"

"He's on his way north to take a job in Wyoming," Cameo explained.

At once Pearl, her features strained, said, "We could pay you, Dan—make it worth your while."

"Actually," Angie added, "we're afraid to go on alone after what happened back at the spring. And with those horrible men still hanging around, and Pa and Uncle Ben both dead, we—"

The woman's voice broke. Sobs choked off her words as tears began to flow. Close by, Lila also began to weep. It was the first sign of grief that Ragan had noticed and he marveled at the strength and control of the Wakefield sisters.

"Won't be no need for pay," he said, tossing aside the cold cigarette butt as he came to a decision. Maybe he'd lose a couple of days, but there was nothing else to do. He sure as hell couldn't just ride off and leave the women to shift for themselves—not while the renegades were still around.

Lila's head came up and a hopeful smile parted her lips. "That mean you'll stay with us till we reach home?"

Ragan said, "Sure does—"

The girl's smile grew wider, and in the pale darkness her eyes seemed to light up. "Wouldn't it be wonderful if we could talk Dan into going to work for us?"

"Wouldn't it though!" Angie added. "He's out of a job—and we need a foreman."

Ragan smiled, shaking his head. "I'm obliged to you, ladies, but I'm sort of set on Wyoming. Besides, I've got to do a fellow a favor along the way. No chance of getting out of that—even if I did change my mind about Wyoming."

"But you will think about it, won't you?" Lila pressed eagerly. "Don't just say no and mean it—not yet. Think about it on the way to the ranch, then when we get there you can look things over and—"

"It's a fine place," Pearl stated, coming into the conversation. "Pa built it up real good—and we've a fine herd—"

"We've got over a thousand head!" Lila broke in.

"And there's better than fifty thousand acres of range, most of it covered with grass—and we've never had any water problems. We have a big garden too, and a lot of fruit trees—so we eat well."

Pearl hesitated and looked questioningly at Ragan, as did the others—all anxiously awaiting his reaction.

"Sounds mighty tempting," Dan admitted, rubbing at his jaw, "and I'll sure do some thinking about it—like Lila there said for me to. But thinking's all I'll do and I don't want to get anybody's hopes up. I gave my word to a dying man that I'd take care of some business for him, and I'm not about to go back on a promise."

"We wouldn't want you to do that," Pearl stated hastily. "But after you've taken care of it—instead of going on to Wyoming —why couldn't you—"

"Like I said, I'll do some thinking about it," Ragan said, rising. "Right now I'm going to mount up and do some looking around—be sure we don't have some company. You all are plenty tired and need some sleep—and you best get it. Tomorrow could be a hard day . . . good night."

"Good night," the women replied quietly, in chorus.

"While you're out there—take care," Cameo, who had remained silent throughout most of the conversation, added. "We don't want anything happening to you, Dan."

Ragan smiled, looked back over his shoulder as he headed for his horse. "Don't fret about that," he said. "I make a habit of being careful."

10

Cameo Wakefield walked slowly across the coulee in deep thought, her eyes on the tall, lean shape of Dan Ragan. She watched him halt beside the big sorrel horse he rode, and noted the graceful, effortless flow of his body as he swung up into the saddle. Half turning as he moved off, he glanced back; seeing her, he smiled and touched the brim of his hat with a forefinger in salute.

A strange sort of gladness was pouring through Cameo. Dan Ragan was one in a million, she told herself, falling back on one of her pa's favorite expressions. Everything about him was big, good, easygoing yet purposeful. He was the kind who knew exactly what he wanted and how to get it—and neither brimstone nor blizzard would keep him from it once he'd set his mind.

Cameo's lips tightened into a wry smile. How could she recognize such values in a man whom she'd known for so short a time? The answer was simple; she was that way herself. They were kindred spirits—and maybe if she handled things right, she just might make them kindred souls! Pivoting leisurely, she returned to the wagon where Angie and Pearl, assisted by Lila, were laying pallets on a canvas tarp.

"I'll say this about him—he sure never wastes any words," the youngest sister was saying as she approached. Then, when she saw Cameo, added: "Oh, I hope we can get Dan to stay, to take a job with us! He's the kind of man I've dreamed of! I—I think I've fallen in love!"

"You forget him!" Cameo said, flatly, and as her two other sisters stopped their work and stared in surprise, continued: "That goes for all of you. He's mine."

Lila's eyes widened. "Yours? How—"

"I think you're both terrible," Pearl declared in a shocked voice. "Pa's lying there in the wagon, dead. And so is Uncle Ben—and here you two are squabbling over a man! It's—it's sacrilege!"

"Pa wouldn't mind," Cameo said with a shrug. "And he was practical enough to know what I've got in mind and why I aim to do it. Wasn't he always preaching at us to be practical?"

"Yes, but with him just dead—not even buried—"

"Oh, pshaw! Be your age, Pearl! We're facing a big problem—and we're going to need help—the good kind that we can trust and depend on."

"And you figure Dan Ragan's the answer?" Angie asked.

"I do. He's just what we've got to have if we're to keep the ranch going. It's too big a job for us to handle alone. Oh, I know we've got hired hands—as good as what comes along—but none of them has the sand to be the boss. Dan Ragan has—I can scc it in him."

"Then, if that's all you want him for—to run the ranch—why can't I have him?" Lila demanded. "He could be our foreman and still be my husband."

Pearl sniffed. "You're moving mighty fast! Why, he hasn't even noticed you, 'specially."

Lila smiled, lowering her head coyly. In the pale light her youthful features were even softer and more beautiful. "I can fix that," she said. "I know how to—"

"I want you to forget him!" Cameo said again, her tone sharp, decisive. "I intend to marry him. Once that's done, our troubles will be over before they can start."

"Marry?" Lila echoed. "But you don't love him—you can't!"

"What's love got to do with it?" Cameo said with a shrug. "Anyway, that'll come later maybe. Main thing is to rope him now, and I figure I'm the most capable of us all to do that."

Lila sat down on the fold of blankets which had not been spread on the tarp. Staring at her hands, locked in her lap, she shook her head. "How can you be so cold-blooded—so heartless? How can you even think of marrying a man you don't love?"

"Mostly because I'm not a romantic ninny like you, with my head all full of silly notions! You see every man that comes along as a story-book knight in shining armor. I see them—him—as a, well, a tool, something to work with, to get a job done with."

"And love has nothing to do with it?" Angie said quietly.

"Nothing—leastwise not now. Important thing to do first off is make the deal—get it all tied down. Love will come later—like I've said."

"Maybe," Pearl said reservedly, "and maybe not. Could be he'll realize you've schemed him into marrying you just so's you'd have a man to run the ranch and look out for you—"

"For us," Cameo broke in. "I'll be doing it for us."

"Then why can't I be the one who—" Lila began protestingly.

"Because you'll never be able to get him—or hold him if he did happen to fall for you. It's a job for a full-grown woman—and that's me."

"It seems to me you're taking a lot for granted," Angie said. "I'd say this Dan Ragan is fair game and there's no good reason why it can't be me or Pearl or Lila. Why must it be you?"

"Because I'm the oldest and the head of the house—if you want the big reason. And I can't risk any of you messing up what is probably our only chance of getting the right man to take over the ranch for us. Another like Dan Ragan might not come along for years!"

Lila, downcast and sullen in the mellow light, brushed at her eyes with the back of a hand. "I still think you've no right to take—"

"I have every right!" Cameo snapped. "I aim to keep the Circle W going no matter what it costs!"

"And who it costs," Angie said pointedly.

"Exactly," Cameo replied coolly. "Now, I don't want to hear any more about it. The matter is closed, and you all are to keep out of my way and let me do what's necessary without any back talk. That understood?"

Cameo fixed her eyes on Lila. The girl nodded petulantly. Angie agreed in a like manner, but Pearl signified her assent with an indifferent shrug.

"All right, it's settled. Now get to bed, all of you—and keep those guns we took off those dead outlaws handy. We just might need them to help Ragan."

Lila got to her feet and began to assist her older sisters with the bedding. Stretching the blankets on the canvas, she glanced briefly at Cameo.

"Aren't you coming to bed too?"

Cameo shook her head, glanced off into the shadow filled grove. "Best I wait up for Dan—show him that I'm concerned about him. Anyway, I must get started. We don't have much time."

Dan Ragan rode slowly off into the grove,

following the dimly visible aisles between the trees and clumps of brush. He headed east, more or less, in the general direction of the spring, reasoning that the three renegades, if they intended to search for the Wakefield girls, and him, would start from that point.

The girls—or rather the women, he reckoned he'd best term them since only the young one, Lila, pretty as a slope of blue asters, could actually be called a girl. The others were pretty, too, but in a different way. All were well built and shapely and of the sort to turn a man's head—and he had yet to get a real good look at them in daylight! He reckoned that the oldest one of the family, Cameo, was about his age, and the prize of the lot.

Ragan halted, listening into the night for any sounds of someone, of a camp close by. The grove, dappled with moon and starlight, was totally silent as even the night birds had hushed.

Dan rode on, eyes drifting back and forth as he searched for signs of the outlaws. It could be they'd had enough—having lost three of their members—and moved out. But somehow he doubted it; the rewards were too tempting and he felt certain they would not move on without making one more attempt to claim the women.

Recalling his earlier conversation with the Wakefields, Dan wondered what it would be like to work for a woman—women to be exact, although the one called Cameo seemed to be the ramrod of the outfit. They'd made him a pretty good offer, one he reckoned he ought to consider taking them up on.

They'd understood about the favor he had to do for Abner Hurley, and how a man had to keep a promise he'd made, and had suggested he go ahead and take care of the matter without even questioning him as to what it was all about. Dan liked that, and it made it easier to consider taking a job on Wakefield's Circle W. Still, he should consider—

Ragan once again drew to a stop, eyes now on a pale glow appearing in the trees not far ahead—a campfire. He moved on, holding the sorrel to a quiet walk until he was but a short distance from the camp. Then dismounting and securing the gelding to a tree, he worked his way in to where he could have a look. It was the renegades whom he'd driven away from the Wake-fields. The three of them were stretched out around the fire, no doubt waiting for daylight at which time they planned to ride on or track down the Wakefield party.

Ragan turned and made his way back to the sorrel. Mounting, he circled the camp with its dying fire until he located the outlaws' horses. Freeing them from their picket ropes, Dan then led them off into the trees, and when finally well away from the sleeping men, released them. Whatever the renegades had planned for the morning would now be delayed while they ran down their mounts.

Satisfied, Ragan cut back through the grove for the wagon and the Wakefield girls. He'd not wait for the sun before he got the party underway. The outlaws had only to locate the tracks of the wagon wheels and start their pursuit; his one chance was to be out of the grove and well on the way with the Wakefields before that occurred.

He reached the coulee where the wagon had halted. The women had gone to bed, he saw as he came down off the sorrel. That was good; he could use a little shut-eye himself, although despite the reassuring sight of the sleeping renegades, he'd still best keep an eye out for them. But that would be no problem; he was a light sleeper.

A slight sound brought Ragan about, his hand dropping instinctively to the pistol on his hip. It fell away as he looked into the face of Cameo Wakefield.

"It's only me," she said, smiling. "I waited up. I just wanted to be sure you were all right."

Dan felt a flush of pleasure and pride as he swung back to the sorrel and began to loosen the cinch and slip the bit. Nobody —especially a woman as attractive as Cameo Wakefield—had ever shown that much interest in his welfare before.

"I'm obliged," he said, finished with the horse and moving back into the center of the swale with her. "Was kind of you."

"That's only part of it," Cameo said softly. "The truth is, you've become very important to me."

11

Ragan slowed, then halted, looking down at Cameo. A frown tugged at the browned planes of his face and corrugated his forehead. She smiled at his puzzlement.

"Don't let this surprise you," she said. "Things between a man and a woman work out this way sometimes—real fast. I think it happened to me when I saw you at the spring standing up to those outlaws—all six of them. Something went through me—a thrill, I guess it was—and a sort of tingling—and there was pride."

"Was no big deal," Dan murmured. "I had the drop on them—caught them cold turkey, in fact."

"Did you see any sign of them?" Cameo asked, apparently believing it best to swiftly change the subject to a less personal one now that the groundwork for their future together had been laid.

He nodded, shifting his glance to the remaining Wakefield women sleeping near the wagon. "They're a mile or so from here—east. Bedded down maybe till daylight, but I'm not banking on it."

"That mean you think we ought to move on right now?"

"Expect we better let the horses rest for a couple more hours. Same goes for your sisters. Then we can hitch up and move out. Come first light I want us to be a far piece from here."

"That's a good idea, all right," Cameo said, agreeing. "But what if they don't wait for first light?"

"Chance we'll be taking," Ragan replied as they continued on into the center of the swale where the wagon stood. "Looked to me like they'd settled down for the night, but there's no for-sure to it."

"Wouldn't our trail be hard for them to find, even if they were hunting for the prints of the wagon wheels? It's strong moonlight, I know, but tracks still won't show up much."

Ragan smiled, pleased at the woman's show of practical knowledge. He looked quickly then to the horses as he stopped at the wagon's tongue and sat down. Something had disturbed them, but he could detect nothing himself. He reckoned it was some small varmint rustling about in the weeds and dry leaves.

"Hadn't you better be getting yourself a mite of rest?" he said, turning to the woman as she found a place beside him on the squared timber.

"I'm not tired—or sleepy," Cameo said. "I'd much rather sit here with you and talk."

Dan changed his position, the movement starting a faint jingle of the trace chains hung over the whiffletrees. He'd never had any association with women of the Wakefield type, his relationships usually being confined to the kind of women found in saloons.

"Can't say I'm long on talk, 'specially with a lady—"

"I don't mind that," Cameo said, and then quickly added, "but maybe you're tired—want to get some sleep."

"No, not that. Expect to stay awake, keep my eyes peeled for those renegades in case they decide to track us down—and find us."

"Then I'll just stay, keep you company,"

Cameo declared, edging close to him as if seeking warmth from the light chill that was settling over the land. "Have you thought any more about my—our offer of a job as foreman on our ranch?"

"Some, not much," Dan admitted, slowly probing the fringe of brush surrounding the coulee with his eyes. "Like I've said, I've already done some promising."

"I realize that, and there's no reason why you can't go ahead, do that favor for your friend. But I don't see why you have to go on to Wyoming. That rancher there won't blame you for taking a better job than he's offering."

Ragan merely nodded. He had seen no signs of movement in the brush or changes in the shadows, but he knew he could take little reassurance from that. It was far more practical to rely on sound rather than sight at such times, and for that reason he wished Cameo Wakefield would go on to bed and leave him to his sentry duties.

"Would it help if I wrote a letter for you to the rancher and explain it all to him?"

Dan Ragan shook his head. Cameo was moving a bit too fast. He hadn't even decided to give up Wyoming yet and here she was rearing to send a letter off to J. J.

Hamilton of the Double J ranch begging him off!

"Can take care of that chore myself," he said, "if it becomes needful."

"Of course!" Cameo said, hastily contrite, evidently realizing she had erred; Dan Ragan's kind would never push a disagreeable task off on somebody else, but as a matter of honor, take care of it themselves—*skin their own polecats,* her pa would say.

"Well, I hope you'll take our offer," Cameo said then. "We talked it over while you were gone and decided you were the man we need—and want. We'll pay whatever wages you want."

"All four of you ladies in on the deciding, or was it just you?" Ragan asked bluntly.

Cameo laughed, a small, merry sound in the cool, clear night. "All of us," she answered, laying a hand on his wrist. "But it's the most important to me—personally, I mean. Do you understand what I'm saying, Dan?"

"Reckon I do," Ragan drawled, "but I best tell you here and now that while I'm right proud you feel like that about me, it's a one way proposition. I ain't—"

"I know it's all on my part, but if you

took the job that would all change, I'm sure. Working together running the ranch like we'd be doing you'd soon feel different about me. Love just sort of develops naturally between a man and a woman when they're together all the time."

Dan was silent for a long minute. Then, "Yeh, I reckon."

Abruptly Cameo straightened, turned and faced him squarely. "I—I never gave it a thought but maybe there's someone else—a girl you plan to marry someday. Or perhaps you already have a wife—somewhere."

Ragan's shoulders stirred. "Nope, neither one. Always been too busy minding my job to think about marrying."

"If you and I got married one day, you'd become a part owner."

It was Dan's turn to twist about. He looked closely at her. "You're carrying me a mite fast, lady! I'm not for certain I—"

"You'll have to forgive me, Dan, but that's the way I am," Cameo said. "When I see something I want, I go after it—same as a man does. Do you think it's wrong for a woman to be like that?'"

"No, I reckon not. Just that I sure'n hell've never run up against a woman like you."

Cameo smiled. "Maybe you've never had a girl fall in love with you before—and tell you so."

"Nope, can't say as I have—"

"And maybe you're not sure it's right. Probably you think it should be the man who does all the pushing."

"Well, yes, ma'am, I reckon that's it."

Cameo looked down. "I—I hope I haven't turned you against me, Dan. I'm a bit forward, I know, but I've always been that way and I can't change."

"No need. Folks have to be what they are."

"I'm glad to hear you say that. Sometimes I worry about what people—the ones I care for anyway—think of me."

"Don't lose no sleep over that, either. You can waste a lot of time fretting over what other folks might think and maybe all the time what they do think ain't worth no more'n a fistful of feathers. Just don't ever let it bother you."

"I know, but sometimes it's important that someone—a special person—thinks the right things about you. This is one of those times, Dan. I want, above everything, for you to think of me in the right way."

"I do," Ragan said politely. "Nothing

you've said or done's going to keep me from knowing you're a fine lady. Can bet on that.''

Cameo heaved a deep sigh. "Thank you, Dan,'' she murmured. "And you will think hard about taking the job I've offered you?''

Ragan nodded absently. His eyes, however, were locked to the brush on the far side of the clearing. A man was standing there looking into the camp. Ragan recognized the checked vest he was wearing. He was one of the renegades.

12

―――――――――

"Easy," Ragan murmured. "We've got company."

Cameo's response was soft, controlled. "Where?"

"Other side of the coulee—near that big clump of oak. One of the renegades that got away."

"I see him. He's wearing a plaid vest. I remember it."

"Yeh," Ragan agreed, slowly changing his position on the wagon tongue. He had misfigured the outlaws; they had not waited for daylight as he'd thought. They had held off until they believed he and the women had made camp and settled down, and then begun their search.

"You see the other two?"

At Cameo's whispered question, Dan

Ragan shook his head. "Nope. Around somewhere close, I suspect. Could be they split up to look for us."

"What can you do? If you shoot—"

"That would be the wrong thing. Would tip off the others to where we are," Ragan said, easing backward off the tongue into the vehicle's deep shadow. "Want you to stay put—like you don't know he's there in case he spots you. I'm going to work around behind him."

Cameo nodded. "Careful—"

Ragan smiled tautly and, moving back deeper into the trees, began a wide circle that would bring him to the rear of the outlaw.

Crouched low, Ragan made his way slowly and quietly through the shadowy grove, keeping always within the dark areas and avoiding the moon- and starlight. There were two more of the renegade party somewhere, and he couldn't afford to let them see him first.

About him the night was hushed, the cool air stilled as if a storm was on the way. Once a rabbit scuttled out from under his booted feet and raced off into the brush. A short time after that an owl, broad wings set, glided silently past in pursuit.

Ragan halted at a thick stand of wild berry

bushes. If he had calculated correctly, he should now be directly in back of the outlaw. There had been no sign of the other two and he reckoned he'd been right in assuming they were elsewhere in the grove searching for the Wakefield wagon.

Drawing his gun, Ragan altered course and began to thread his way through the trees toward the coulee. Abruptly he stopped. The dark silhouette of the outlaw, standing at the edge of the clearing, was before him.

The man was motionless as he studied the camp, the wagon and the sleeping women nearby. He could not see the horses drawn up in a line a bit to the left, nor was Cameo visible to him. Likely he was getting the camp's arrangement fixed in his mind, after which he would rejoin his partners and the three of them would close in.

He'd best wait no longer, Ragan decided; the missing outlaws, unsuccessful elsewhere in the grove, could put in their appearance at any time. Pistol gripped firmly in his hand, Dan moved forward silently through the brush. A stride behind the outlaw he raised his arm. At that moment the renegade, either hearing some slight sound or sensing Ragan's presence, wheeled. Dan swung the forty-five with all his strength. It caught the outlaw on the side of the head, dropping him where he stood.

Ragan remained poised, coiled, listening into the night. The solid thud and the crackling of brush as the renegade went down had seemed loud, and if the man's friends were near, Ragan was certain they had heard.

But several minutes later, reassured that the noise had gone unnoticed, Dan holstered his pistol, and stepping up to the crumpled figure of the man, he relieved him of the gun he was wearing and hurled it off into the brush.

Taking the outlaw's bandanna, he tied it tight across his mouth to prevent his calling out, and then, stripping off the cartridge belt, secured the fellow's hands behind his back. Leaving the still unconscious renegade thus helpless, Ragan continued to circle the coulee, alert for any indications that the two remaining outlaws were near. He discovered nothing, and returning to the clearing, he found Cameo waiting where he had left her—on the tongue of the wagon.

She came to her feet at once when she saw him, a smile of relief on her lips. "You're all right!" she said in a breathless sort of way.

"When I didn't hear anything I was afraid something had gone wrong. What—"

"Knocked him cold, then gagged and tied him. Won't have to worry about him for a while," Ragan replied. "No sign of the others. Expect we best hitch up and get out of here. They're bound to start looking for their partner."

Cameo considered him. "I wouldn't be afraid of them—not after seeing the way you handled them earlier. Was six then—now there'll be only two. You could shoot—"

"Killing a man's bad business—outlaw or not," Ragan said, glancing at the sleeping women. "I've made a rule to never use my gun unless there's no other answer. Wake up your sisters and get ready to move out. I'll get the horses."

Within a half hour they were leaving the grove and moving into the low hill country to the west. There was no road or trail, and Ragan, handling the lines with the sorrel tied to the wagon's tailgate and following along reluctantly, chose a direct, straight course regardless of how rough.

Cameo sat beside him and for the first hour few words passed between them. The remaining Wakefield sisters, occupying the seats built crosswise in the wagon's bed, were silent also, preferring to doze as the vehicle rocked and jolted along on its due-west journey.

First light found them well away from the trees. The team, rested to some extent, was steady, if slow, and showed no signs of tiring. Ragan, however, was unwilling to press them and at full daylight pulled up in a hollow between two hills.

"Got to blow the horses," he explained. "And I want to see if there's anybody on our trail."

Cameo nodded her understanding, and then added: "Will we have time to make coffee?"

Dan glanced at the women standing in a line before him waiting for his answer. In that moment he was having his first good look at the Wakefields. Lila, the youngest, with dark hair and blue eyes, was the prettiest of all, although her sisters were equally well built.

Angie, a blonde with brown eyes, probably in her early twenties, had a sweet way about her that set her somewhat apart. Pearl was much like her—also a blonde, brown-eyed woman a bit younger, perhaps, but with a certain prudishness that reminded Dan of a schoolteacher he had once met.

Cameo, like Lila, had dark hair and blue eyes and a well-turned figure, but there the similarity ended. Instead of the delicate beauty of the younger girl, she possessed a firmness and a capability that plainly bespoke her position as the head of the family. That she could take care of herself —and others if necessary—was clearly evident.

"Coffee, maybe," he said, "but keep the fire low. Don't want any smoke telling where we are."

Cameo wheeled immediately to Angie. "Get the pot and the sack of coffee beans," she said, and then to Lila and Pearl: "You two fetch some wood—and be sure it's good and dry."

The three moved off at once to do their bidden chores, making no comment. Ragan, nodding crisply to Cameo, also turned and, walking hurriedly, climbed to the crest of the nearest hill. Keeping a clump of brush between himself and the now distant grove, he shaded his eyes with a cupped hand and studied the undulating land before him.

The only signs of life were a long-eared jackrabbit moving leisurely along the base of a nearby bluff and a red-tailed hawk circling high overhead. The outlaw he had left trussed and gagged hadn't been able to free himself as yet, Dan reckoned, nor had his friends located him.

That was good. He had a long start on them despite the slow-moving wagon and with a bit more of the right kind of luck could hold the lead. But once the renegades got themselves organized and found the prints of the wagon's wheels, they could set out in pursuit and trim his lead in short time.

The Wakefield women not only had coffee ready when he returned but had taken advantage of the small fire to warm over a few biscuits and some of the dried meat they had in the provision box. Cameo and her sisters had already satisfied their hunger, and bolting down a bit of the food and two cups of the strong, black coffee, Ragan took care of his needs. He was more interested in putting greater distance between himself and the grove than in eating.

Noon found them well out in the broken hill country and now bearing slightly south on a faintly defined but good road that made traveling much easier for the team. Dan still held the reins and Cameo had not forsaken her place beside him on the seat.

All during the long miles now she

maintained a steady conversation, sometimes with him, on other occasions with her sisters. Usually it had to do with the ranch—the things they should or should not do—all the while making it clear that he was a part of the future and their plans.

Ragan was puzzled. He had made no commitment to Cameo Wakefield. He began to wonder now if the eldest Wakefield sister had led the others to a different conclusion, that as soon as he had fulfilled the promise he'd made Abner Hurley he would return to the Circle W and assume duties that would develop later, Angie had coyly intimated, into a more lasting and prominent position.

Finally, when it reached the point where the girls were planning to rearrange their father's room for his use, Ragan felt it was time to call a halt to such talk.

"Ladies, this deal of me taking on the job as your ramrod's sort of getting out of hand," he said, getting their attention. "I don't know what's got you to thinking it's all cut and dried, because it sure ain't. I promised to do some thinking about it—and that's all."

Lila leaned forward on her seat, bracing herself against the rocking of the wagon with one hand gripping the side of the box.

"You mean you haven't said you'd take the job?"

"No, he hasn't," Cameo replied before Ragan could shape an answer. "Said he'd think about it after he'd taken care of that other matter—that favor he feels is so mighty important. But the offer sounds good to him—he's as much as said so. Isn't that right, Dan?"

"Said it was plenty tempting," Ragan admitted. He was staring ahead, eyes on a cloud of dust rising from beyond a distant hogback a bit to their left. Riders. Or it could be cattle on the move. "But I'm not saying for sure one way or another. . . . There another ranch around here somewheres?"

Cameo frowned. "No—not for miles. Ours is the only one—and it's not far."

Ragan pointed to the thin yellow cloud. "Would that be some of your stock being moved?"

The eldest Wakefield studied the dust for several moments. She shook her head. "Couldn't be. Too far east—and anyway we drift our stock to the north this time of year for new grass."

Ragan immediately passed the reins to her. "Reckon I'd best get my horse. Now, if we run into trouble, don't stop—just keep driving."

Cameo said something to him but he did not hear what it was, nor did he trouble to find out. Dropping from the still moving wagon, he circled to its rear, and trotting alongside the sorrel, freed him from the lead rope tied to the bridle. As the big gelding slowed, Ragan grasped the lines and, one hand on the horn, swung up onto the saddle. Immediately he spurred out in front of the team and wagon.

The cloud of dust had disappeared. Puzzled, Dan considered the empty sky above the ridge. It could not have been a herd of drifting cattle, he reasoned; if the cowhands tending it had brought it to a halt, there would still be dust. Cattle were a restless lot and constantly milled about. There was only one explanation: riders.

But he saw no indication of such in the hours that followed and as the afternoon wore on under the increasing heat of the sun, Ragan began to feel better about the rene-gades. Most likely, just as Peabody and his men had apparently done, they had given up and turned to other things. It was a relief to be rid of them and the threat they posed.

Brushing his hat to the back of his head,

Dan swiped at the sweat on his face with a deep sigh. He settled slackly in his saddle. Half turning, he reached around and laid his hand on the black saddlebags containing the money he'd pledged to deliver to May Hurley in the town of Blackwater. It would be a hell of a big relief to rid himself of that, too! It seemed months since he'd been able to draw an easy breath, although it was less than a week that he'd assumed the responsibility first of Hurley's money, and then the welfare and safety of the Wakefield women.

But he'd soon be shed of both—the women even before sunset, Hurley's cash within a couple of days. Then he would have to make his decision as to the future. Would it be on to Wyoming and the job of foreman on J. J. Hamilton's ranch, or back to Wakefield's Circle W to take a like job —only with more import as to the future! He—

Ragan's thoughts stalled. Anger whipped impatiently through him; he'd figured wrong again where the renegades were concerned. Coming from behind a low hill in a three-pronged approach, they were headed right for him!

13

Cursing savagely, Ragan wheeled and raced back to the wagon. Veering in close, he pointed to the outlaws.

"Whip up the team! I'll try to keep them away!"

Cameo nodded, and as Ragan swung off, he saw her change places with one of her sisters—either Angie or Pearl, he couldn't be certain which. He gave brief wonder why she would hand the reins over to someone else when she undoubtedly was the most expert, but the thought was short; the renegades had already opened up on him with their guns.

Simmering at the situation in which he found himself, Dan drew his weapon. Hunched low over the sorrel's neck, he spurred toward the renegades. He saw that only two of the outlaws were firing at him.

Evidently the checked-vest man he'd knocked unconscious and left bound and gagged in the grove had never found his pistol.

Regan flinched as a bullet struck the horn of his saddle and screamed off into space. Instantly he cut hard left, and steadying himself as best he could, triggered a shot at the nearest renegade. The man stiffened and rocked back in his saddle—hit but apparently not badly wounded. Dan saw him shift his gun from right to left hand, and reckoned the bullet had only disabled an arm.

The rattle of gunfire was constant now, and dust mixing with powder smoke was beginning to drift across the flat. Ragan took aim again and pressed off a load, but the movement of the sorrel as he swerved abruptly to avoid a clump of brush spoiled the shot. Dan tried again, swearing as the hammer clicked on an empty shell. Still hunched low, allowing the reins to hang from the horn and the gelding to run free, he hurriedly reloaded

The forty-five ready once more, Dan twisted about and flung a glance at the wagon. It was swinging from side to side as it raced along the road; from beneath its arched top at the rear, Cameo and Lila, crouched, were shooting at the outlaws with the pistols they had taken from the bodies of the dead outlaws back at the spring.

It was apparent that the women lacked much where accuracy with a pistol was concerned, and he had doubts they were familiar at all with such weapons, but their shooting was having some effect, as the renegades no longer were coming straight at them, and had altered course and were now riding parallel.

Dan's fear for the women heightened. They were much easier targets now. Grim, he deliberately cut away from the wagon and rode directly for the nearest outlaw. The sorrel, running at top speed, carried him in close. He was within easy range almost before the renegade became aware of his intention. The man, finally hearing the drumming of the big horse's hoofs, whirled. His mouth sagged as surprise shocked him. He whipped his pistol about to fire a quick shot. Ragan, already set, triggered his weapon.

The outlaw buckled as the bullet drove into him. Immediately his horse veered off, slowing as the hand holding the reins tightened. The animal swerved again, came to a stiff-legged halt. The renegade pitched forward and fell heavily to the ground.

Spurring on past the stricken man, Ragan brought his gun to bear on the next renegade. He fired, missed. Cocking the weapon once more, he again drew bead—he paused. A frown pulled at his taut features. The remaining two outlaws had abruptly swung off, racing back in the direction of the distant grove.

Slowing the heaving sorrel Dan turned back to rejoin the Wakefields, reloading his pistol as he crossed the fairly short expanse of mesa. When he drew nearer to the wagon, now at a stop, he saw Cameo and Lila drop to the ground and hurry forward to meet him.

They were all right. Relief flowed through him and he shifted his attention to the front of the vehicle, to Angie and Pearl. He stiffened slightly when he saw them looking ahead—down the road. Four riders were in sight and approaching fast. Dan, in the act of holstering his pistol, brought it up once again. More trouble.

"No!" Cameo called to him as he cut in beside the team and prepared to meet the riders. "They're from the ranch—they work for us!"

Ragan grinned tightly and slid his gun into

its holster. Those men would never know how welcome they were, for their arrival meant that he need worry no more about the Wakefield sisters' safety—and he could go on about his own business.

Swinging off the sweaty sorrel, Dan walked up to where Cameo was standing. The four Circle W men had halted on the opposite side of the wagon and were in conversation with Lila. Pulling off his hat, he nodded.

"Reckon this about winds up things for me," he said. "Figure I best be on my way."

Cameo's face clouded, and from the seat of the vehicle, Pearl said: "Won't you at least come on to the ranch with us, let us show you how much we appreciate what—"

"Dan knows what he has to do first," Cameo cut in sharply. "You know he has that favor to do for a friend. When that's taken care of—"

The woman hesitated, looking directly at Ragan as if waiting for him to make a comment. Nearby the cowhands from the ranch had moved to the rear of the wagon and were having their look at the dead men under the blanket. When no response came from Dan, Angie voiced her feelings.

"I hope you realize how grateful we are to

you," she said. "If it hadn't been for you we—"

"Was proud to help," Ragan said bluntly. "And I'm mighty glad things've turned out right, 'cepting, of course, for your pa and your uncle."

Cameo motioned the cowhands back to their horses and then turned to Dan. "You'll be back as soon as you take care of that favor, won't you?"

"Not for sure yet," Ragan said, moving back to the sorrel gelding. "Fact is, there's been so much of a hooraw I haven't had time to think much about anything. Now that you folks are safe, I reckon I can start."

"Then I—we'll hear from you later?" Cameo pressed, following him to his horse and standing close by while he mounted. "Within a few days? We can't wait long."

He gave that thought as he settled himself in his saddle. Finally he shifted his glance to the other Wakefield sisters, nodded, and then brought his attention back to Cameo. It was evident he was keeping matters on as impersonal a basis as possible.

"One way or another. . . . So long, ladies," he said and, touching the brim of his hat with a forefinger, he wheeled the sorrel about and rode off.

Near sundown two days later, Ragan caught sight of Ed Peabody and his three partners. Upon leaving the Wakefield sisters he had followed a slanting course, one designed to bring him eventually back to the north trail. It had worked out just that way, he having come to the primary road the following midafternoon.

The outlaws had continued northward, and that puzzled Dan somewhat, since it was likely they did not know where Abner Hurley lived. And then it came to him that they were simply searching for him. Having lost him somewhere in the area east of the grove, they had pressed their hunt in the direction he had been going—north. But they were of no consequence now; he was well ahead of them and would have reached Blackwater and moved on by the time they arrived. He reckoned losing them was one of the good things that had come from helping the Wakefield sisters; it had taken him far off course, and that had thoroughly confused and delayed Peabody and the others.

The Wakefields . . . Dan was uncertain as to what his decision would be once he rid himself of Hurley's money, and, curiously, he was reluctant to even think about it. He continually put it from his mind each time the subject occurred to him, and as he drew nearer to the settlement, it became apparent to him that he must soon make his choice.

Taking over as foreman for J. J. Hamilton on his Wyoming spread would be a fine thing to do; it would be a big job, one where he would have no responsibilities other than seeing to the care of cattle. On the other hand, at Wakefield's Circle W, he would be more than just the foreman. It was clear the women expected him to take over the complete running of their ranch—and in time become a member of the family!

Dan swiped at the sweat on his forehead and scrubbed at the whiskers on his chin. That first part would be just fine—being the bull of the woods—the top-hand boss of a ranch; it would be like having his own outfit, doing things the way he wanted them done, running the place exactly as he saw fit. But the second part of the deal—the marrying up with Cameo Wakefield which undoubtedly was a part of the bargain—he wasn't so sure about that. He'd sure have to do some tall thinking before he picked that course!

Dan glanced ahead through the late afternoon heat haze. He was figuring he'd have plenty of time yet to mull it over, but then as he topped out a low hill, he realized he'd run out of time insofar as a decision was concerned. Directly below him, in a valley covered with range grass and studded with trees and brush, lay the town. Its name evidently had been taken from a small lake of dark looking water which lay off to the right.

BLACKWATER 1 MILE a sign advised a short time later when he reached the foot of the slope. Dan halted there, stirring restlessly on the saddle as a vague uneasiness moved through him. He had seen—or thought he'd seen—motion in the brush bordering the road.

He remained quiet, listening and probing the undergrowth with his glance for several minutes. Then, neither seeing nor hearing any further indication of possible trouble, he drew his gun and, holding it in his lap, started the sorrel forward once again. The big gelding covered a dozen yards and then drew up abruptly of its own accord. Three men had ridden out of the brush and were blocking his way.

14

"Pull up there—and raise your hands!"

It was the man in the center who had spoken out in a hard voice. About thirty, he was fairly well dressed, with small, darting eyes, light hair, and a close-clipped mustache.

Ragan smiled tautly and lifted the weapon he was holding slightly. It was pointed directly at the speaker.

"No, I reckon not," he drawled.

He let his glance touch the other men. One was a squat individual, redheaded and with a hard set to his florid face. The other was slim and dark and wore among other items a black leather vest adorned with silver conchos and two pistols holstered in crossed gunbelts.

"Name's Sutton," said the blond with a

deep frown. "Can see you're new around here, else you'd know I'm the law."

"Law?" Ragan echoed skeptically. He could think of no reason why the law would stop him.

"Deputy sheriff," Sutton said, and digging into a pocket of his shirt held up a star to verify his statement. "These boys are pals of mine. Redhead there's Bob Swinnerton. Other fellow's Cully Greer. They sort of work as deputies, too, when I'm needing help."

"Where's the sheriff?" Dan asked, not relenting.

"Up north a piece. This ain't the county seat so he don't hang around here much. Leaves it to me to look after things."

Ragan continued to study the three men. Sutton could be a deputy, although the fact that he had a badge to prove it meant nothing. A man could buy himself a star at just about any gun shop. And Greer and Swinnerton—they looked like any of the cowhands he'd seen hanging around the offices of lawmen hoping to pick up a few dollars serving on posses and doing other odd jobs. Likely they were what they claimed to be—but Dan was not convinced. Why had they stopped him? And so far he hadn't been asked to identify himself, which was what you'd expect if they were hunting for someone.

"What do you want with me?" he asked.

Sutton pointed to the black saddlebags on Ragan's sorrel. "Ab Hurley's money," he said. "Ain't for certain what you're doing with it but I can see you got it. You going to say you ain't?"

Ragan shook his head. "Nope, I've got it. How'd you know about it?"

"Ab's a friend of mine. Sent a letter to his woman that he was coming home with a pile of money—"

"And that's who I'm handing it over to—his wife," Dan cut in flatly. "Promised Hurley before he died that I'd do it."

Sutton glanced at Swinnerton and then at Greer. "So Ab's dead. Figured that when I seen you with his saddlebags. You kill him?"

"Hell, no!" Ragan replied hotly. "You think I'd be toting all that money across country to his wife if I had? He got shot up by some outlaws."

"Yeh, makes sense," Sutton said after a few moments' consideration. "Well, you've done what you told him you'd do. Can give me the money and I'll take it to May."

Sutton had called Hurley's wife by name.

Dan reckoned that should be proof enough of the man's sincerity. However, that wasn't the deal he'd made the dying rancher.

"Obliged, but Hurley made me promise to hand it over to his wife—and nobody else. Expect that's how it's going to be." He paused, a thought coming to him, one aroused by still unsatisfied suspicion. "How'd you happen to be waiting here for me? How'd you know I was coming?"

Sutton shrugged, brushing at his mustache. "Was expecting Ab a couple of days ago. He didn't show up and May got sort of worried. Asked me to look for him—there's been a right smart of holdups and such around here lately. Me and the boys was aiming to head south this evening if Ab hadn't rode in."

Ragan slid his pistol into its holster in a gesture of acceptance. He reckoned carrying all that money, the encounter with Peabody and his crowd, and the renegades he'd been forced to shoot it out with had all served to make him a bit too edgy.

"All right," he said, "you can take me to May Hurley now."

"Like I've told you, you can turn the money over to me. I'll see she gets it," Sutton snapped impatiently.

Dan's hand was again resting on the butt of his forty-five. "I aim to do just what I promised Hurley."

"Hell with him, Will!" Swinnerton said, breaking his silence and edging forward a few steps on his horse. "You ain't getting nowheres arguing with this bullhead. Whyn't you just take them saddlebags and—"

"No need to get tough, Bob," Sutton cut in, raising a hand. "The man made a promise and wants to keep it. I can't fault him none for that. Come on—say, what is your name, anyway, cowboy? Don't recollect you giving it."

"Wasn't asked," Dan replied. "It's Ragan—Dan Ragan."

"All right, Ragan. Follow me. I'll take you right to May's house."

The deputy wheeled about and struck off down the road in the direction of the settlement. Ragan sat motionless, waiting for Swinnerton and Greer to swing into line, electing not to move until they had.

Sutton pursued a course that circled the town. Their trail came out finally in a clearing that once had been a farm on the town's eastern side. Near the forward edge of the open ground, now ravaged by weeds and other rank growth, a small house had been built. Lonely and deserted-appearing, it showed no signs of care—or even of present occupancy.

"Looks like May ain't home," Sutton observed as they pulled to a halt at the sagging hitch rack and dismounted.

Suspicion had again risen in Dan Ragan, and his hand once more hovered near the gun on his hip. "Don't look to me like she or anybody else is living here," he said.

"The Hurleys ain't been here long—it was a sort of temporary arrangement," Sutton explained, crossing to the door. Pushing it open, he yelled: "May? You in there?"

There was no reply. Sutton beckoned to Ragan. "Best you come on in and wait. May's somewheres in town, I expect. I'll go fetch her."

Ragan gave that thought and then, turning to the sorrel, lifted the Mexican saddlebags off his hull, hung them over a shoulder and walked toward the house. His hand was now riding the butt of his pistol and he was sharply alert for any wrong move on the part of Will Sutton and the pair with him as he slowly crossed the littered yard.

"Just you go right on in, make yourself to home," Sutton said, waving at the open doorway. "If you're hungry look around the kitchen a bit. Be some grub in there somewheres and May sure ain't going to mind your helping yourself after what you're doing for her."

Dan said nothing, and climbing the two warped and splintered steps to the landing that fronted the cabin, he entered. He had been wrong, he saw, in thinking the place was not being lived in. There were dishes in a pan on the stove, rumpled blankets on the bed, and a number of boxes, cans and sacks of foodstuff on the shelves, all of which bore out Sutton's declaration.

"Bob and Cully'll stick around here with you," Dan heard the deputy say. "I won't be gone more'n a few minutes."

Ragan strode to the far side of the large room, and, hanging the saddlebags across the back of a chair, sat down facing the doorway. The job wasn't over yet as far as he was concerned—not until he'd handed the money to Abner Hurley's wife. Silent, still wary, he watched Swinnerton and Greer enter, but they paid little attention to him, simply finding themselves places at the table in the corner of the room that served as a kitchen and settling down.

Sutton was as good as his word. Within a quarter hour he returned, bringing with him a middle-aged blonde who still showed traces of her youthful beauty. The deputy introduced her as May Hurley, and Ragan, after being further convinced of her identity when shown the letter the rancher had sent her, placed the saddlebags of money in her hands.

Dry-eyed she listened to his account of what had happened, and when he had finished, she smiled sadly. "It was kind of you to help Ab. I'm glad there was somebody with him when he died."

Dan nodded. "If you'd like to see where he's buried, I'll fix you a map—"

"No need," May said. "He's dead and gone and going there won't do him no good—or me, either."

May Hurley was taking it all very well, Dan realized, although she was probably in a state of shock and the worst was yet to come for her. He stepped back and, hat off, smiled at her.

"Want to say how sorry I am to be bringing you bad news like this, but I'm proud I could do what your husband asked."

"It was kind of you," the woman said again, laying the saddlebags on the table. "If there's anything I can do for you—"

"Nope, nothing. I'm fine, thanks. And I expect I'd best be heading out now," Ragan said, backing toward the door.

Sutton moved up and offered his hand. "I'm hoping you ain't holding no grudge against me. Was only doing my job."

"No hard feelings," Ragan said, taking the man's fingers into his own. Then, nodding briefly to all, he murmured *"Adios,"* wheeled, and stepped out onto the landing.

He felt as if a huge load had slipped from his shoulders, and when he swung up onto the sorrel, cut the big gelding about, and headed off down the trail, he had an urge to yell to physically express his relief. He was done with the promise he'd made Abner Hurley—he had delivered the money just as he'd said he would—and now all he had to stew about was which of the jobs he'd been offered he should take. It was a great feeling to be free again with no worries, no responsibilities, no thoughts other than to decide which of the foreman jobs was better for him—

Ragan cursed suddenly and jerked the sorrel to a halt. For the second time that day riders had pulled out in front of him to block his way. But with these men he was familiar; it was Ed Peabody and his outlaw partners.

15

"He ain't got the saddlebags—"

It was the one Hurley had named Rufe Cobb, the rider of a white-stockinged black horse. The man was slight and wiry, wearing leather pants and a fringed deerskin jacket.

Peabody was Cobb's opposite in appearance—big, thick-shouldered, black-bearded, and wearing ordinary range clothing. Leaning forward on the gray, he rested one hand on the horn of his saddle and glared at Dan through small, agate-hard eyes.

"Where's the money? What the hell'd you do with it?"

Ragan let his glance touch the pistols being leveled at him by Dave Kitchens and the outlaw called Arlie Redd. A half smile pulled at Dan's lips.

"You're too late—"

"Too late!" Peabody echoed. "The hell we are! I want to know what you've done with it!"

"He's gone and cached it somewheres, Ed," Cobb said. "I'll take my rope and drag him through the brush a bit—that'll sure make him talk."

"No point in that," Dan said coolly. "I ain't got it—and I never hid it."

Cobb reached down and began to untie the leather string that held his rope to the saddle. "Ain't no sense wasting time on this jasper. When I get done with him he'll—"

"Forget it, Rufe," Peabody said, glancing about at the others. "I figure he don't know who he's dealing with. He'll talk or he'll go to jail."

Ragan frowned. "You saying you're the law?"

"Sheriff from over Texas way. These men are my deputies," Peabody said. "We've been chasing that damned Hurley for a week—ever since he held up a trail boss and took a pile of money off him."

Dan shrugged. "That's not the way I got the story."

"I ain't giving a damn what you've heard!" Peabody said, shifting angrily on his saddle. "Here's the straight of it: Ab Hurley

132

and three of his sidekicks held up a trail boss the day after the fellow'd sold off his herd. Killed him doing it.

"We happened to be close and got rung in on it. Took out after them and the bunch split up, but we seen that Hurley was the one with the money—seen him stuffing it in his saddlebags—so we followed him."

"Chased him across half of Texas and was getting close when that sandstorm hit us and we lost him. Know he was some shot up because just before he give us the slip we threw some lead at him. Seen him damn nigh fall off his horse. Was bad hurt."

Ragan listened in silence. These men were all outlaws, if he was to believe Abner Hurley—yet Peabody claimed to be a lawman and the men with him his deputies. A disturbing thought ran through Dan; could he have been taken in, made a sucker by Hurley? Had he been dodging lawmen instead of outlaws all the way from the shack where he'd met Hurley? It seemed hardly possible.

"I ain't swallowing that," he said stubbornly. "What Hurley told me makes more sense."

"What'd he tell you?" Peabody demanded.

"That the money was his. That he was a rancher and he'd sold out his place and was on his way home when the four of you jumped him. Far as I'm concerned, that's the truth."

Peabody laughed and, drawing his gun, pointed it at Dan's head. "The hell you say! Now, climb down off that horse—and keep your hands up. I ain't got time to take you back to jail, so maybe Rufe's idea of making you talk'll be a good idea. You hear? Climb down!"

Ragan, mindful of the warning since there were now three pistols leveled at him, swung off the sorrel slowly. Doubt was beginning to cloud his mind now, to shake his conviction. Could Peabody be what and who he claimed to be? Had Hurley taken him in—made a fool of him?

"That's sure a good joke—old Ab telling this greenhorn he was a rancher," Kitchens observed with a laugh. "He ain't never done a honest day's work in his life!"

"Ain't it the truth," Rufe Cobb agreed, shaking the loops out of his rope. He turned his eyes on Ragan. "Mister, you've been hornswoggled good! Yes, sir—mighty good! I'm betting you're new around here."

"Ab Hurley ain't no rancher," Peabody

134

said. "And he never was. Just a two-bit gambler and cardsharp. He was plain lying if he told you something else." The big man paused, and gun still in hand, folded his arms across his chest.

"Now, cowboy," he continued, "I sure don't want to get mean with you, but like I said I ain't got time to tote you back to Texas so I'm wanting some answers right here and now—and I aim to get them.

"Being the sheriff of the county where this all happened makes it my business to straighten out killings and holdups and such—but I want to do it right, and I sure don't want to make it hard on an innocent man."

"And we know Ab give you the money before he cashed in," Arlie Redd stated.

"Who said he died?" Ragan countered.

"Now, don't go handing us that bull!" Peabody said with a curse. "We spotted that cabin where you and him holed up. We seen all the blood on the floor, and it didn't take no coon hound to snuff out where you buried him."

"And then we spotted you heading north with them Mex saddlebags of his'n," Kitchens added. "We got you dead to rights so you best start talking up to Ed—to the sheriff.''

Peabody nodded thoughtfully, scratched at his beard. ''That's for sure, but I'm thinking something else. Maybe you was in on the killing and holdup with Ab and them others. I'm remembering now that you kept giving us the slip all the time we was chasing you—like you plain didn't want to get caught up with.''

''Far as I knew you were outlaws after Hurley's money,'' Ragan said. ''That's what he told me—and I'm not so sure yet that it's not the truth. You got a star or something that'll prove you're who you say you are?''

Peabody frowned, glancing about at the others. ''Any of you boys think to wear your deputy badge? I lost my star when we was bucking that damn sandstorm—and I sure ain't carrying no papers. Never've had to show nobody nothing before, being well known back in Texas—and far as a badge is concerned, they're a dime a dozen.''

''Being out of Texas—and out of your county, your badge'd be no good here anyway. I know enough about the law to realize that—''

''Maybe you think you do, but lawmen all sort of work together—'specially when there's been a killing. But you ain't got around to answering my question."

Ragan lowered his hands, struggling in his mind to decide whether Peabody was telling him the truth—which, if so, would mean that Hurley had lied, and further, that he had turned the money over to Hurley's bunch. It was beginning to look as if he'd done just that, but Dan wasn't ready to admit it just yet.

"Question? What question?"

"Dammit—you know what question!" Peabody snarled. "Said I was wondering if you was in on the holdup, and maybe was a part of—"

"No," Ragan cut in quickly, "I just happened to be in the cabin when Hurley, all shot up, came in. Made me promise to take the money to his wife—she lives here in Blackwater. Told me to watch out for you, that you were outlaws aiming to take the money from him."

Peabody gave that consideration. Then, "Maybe so. Anyway, I'll swallow it. Where's the money?"

"I handed it over to Hurley's wife like he wanted me to do," Ragan replied.

Peabody swore—a lengthy, low-breath string of fiery oaths. When he had vented his anger, he holstered his weapon, pulled off his hat, and swiping at the sweat on his forehead, glared at Dan Ragan.

"All right, you done handed the money over to Hurley's wife. Ain't nothing I can do about that now. How'd you find her?"

Ragan shrugged. He had been a fool—an out-and-out, twenty-four-carat-gold sucker—when he let Abner Hurley talk him into delivering the stolen money to his wife, who evidently was no less an outlaw than he. Now Dan was wondering about Will Sutton, Greer, and Bob Swinnerton; were they really lawmen as they claimed to be, or were they the other members of the Hurley outlaw gang?

"Three men stopped me at the edge of town. One was a deputy sheriff. Said they were friends of Ab Hurley's and were getting ready to go looking for him."

"Three? You say three men?" Peabody asked, leaning forward.

"Yeh, three. Was one—"

"You hear their names?"

"The deputy—he showed me a badge—called himself Will Sutton. The others—"

"Sutton!" Rufe Cobb exploded. "That lousy little cardsharp! He ain't no deputy—he's one of Hurley's bunch. He was

138

with him when he killed that trail boss."

"Them other two didn't happen to be Cully Greer and Bob Swinnerton, did they?" Kitchens added.

Ragan swore wearily as he nodded. Sutton and the two others had taken him in, too —just as Hurley had! What the hell was wrong with him? Was he just plain dumb?

He became aware of Peabody's continuing, intent stare. There was a smirk on the big man's heavy features now.

"I'm betting you're the all time champion greenhorn!" Peabody said finally. "Hell, Sutton and them two others ain't lawmen. They probably had it all cooked up with Ab to meet him and his wife here—"

"That wife!" Rufe Cobb declared contemptuously. "She's tougher'n any six men I know—all rolled into one."

"None of them are strangers to you, I take it."

"They sure ain't. Know them from 'way back," Ed Peabody said. "Penny-ante road agents, cardsharps, two-bit gamblers. Ain't nothing much at anything. Was it them that showed you where May Hurley was?"

Ragan nodded. "Took me to a house where they said she was living. Wasn't there and I had to wait while Sutton went to find her.''

"Why didn't they just take that money away from you?'' Kitchens said. "Cully Greer ain't the kind to let some greenhorn keep him from getting what he's after— 'specially if it's a lot of cash.''

"Could be because I spotted them in the brush first and was holding a gun on Sutton all the time,'' Ragan said, a bit stiffly.

Kitchens laughed. "You got the drop on that big four-flusher, eh? Well, yellow like he is, I expect that changed things aplenty!''

"So they took you to this here shack,'' Peabody pressed impatiently. "May show up right away?''

"Was a few minutes. Not long.''

"Then you handed the money over to her?''

"Yeh, like I promised Hurley I'd do. Gave it straight to her, nobody else.''

Kitchens put his gun away, drew out the makings, and began to roll a cigarette. Somewhere over in the direction of the town a dog began to bark. "Old May was making for sure she'd get her share. If you'd give it to Sutton and them others she'd probably never seen a dime of it.''

"Well, far as I'm concerned there ain't

none of them going to get any of it," Ed Peabody stated flatly. "Mister, I want you to take us to that shack where you met her. Could be they'll still be there. Reckon you can find it again?"

There was a trace of irony in Peabody's voice. Anger lifted in Ragan and for a moment he was tempted to tell the Texas lawman to go to hell, to find the house where May Hurley lived himself; and then the feeling of embarrassment, of guilt at having been a party in aiding a bunch of killers to evade the law, brushed the temptation aside. He'd do what he could to make things right, and then move on, put it all behind him.

"Sure," he said, his tone abrupt. Moving by Cobb, still fiddling with his rope, Ragan swung up onto his horse. Wheeling the sorrel about, Dan started back up the trail with Peabody and his deputies following in single file.

When they came to the clearing in which the house sat, Peabody called a halt. "Best we keep out of sight, leastwise till we get all set," he said. "Sutton and them ain't going to be easy to take."

"Can be damn sure of that," Redd agreed. He was a man given to few words and had spoken but little since Ragan had met him. "Who all's in there?"

"Told you that," Ragan replied indifferently, and pointed to the three horses standing at the hitch rack. "Sutton, Greer, and Swinnerton. And the woman—May Hurley."

"And there ain't nobody else?"

"Not unless somebody's come since I walked out an hour or so ago."

"That ain't likely," Peabody said. "Was only four of them to start with in the holdup—counting Hurley. Wouldn't be no outsider showing up now. . . . Which way you riding from here?" he added, turning his attention to Dan.

"North—Wyoming, far as I know."

"Ain't you for sure?" Cobb asked, grinning. "Seems a man ought to—"

"Had a job offered to me on a ranch west of here," Ragan cut in. "Just might take it instead."

"I reckon you're all fixed up then," Peabody said, "so you might as well be on your way."

"Ed's right," Cobb added. "Ain't no point in you hanging around here no longer. It's up to us lawmen to handle things now, and we sure would hate to see you get hit with a stray bullet when the shooting starts."

Ragan nodded, agreeing. It would be as big a relief to get away from the mess he'd made as it had been to rid himself of the money—and it was all because he'd made a promise to a dying man.

"I'll be moving on then," he said, cutting the sorrel around. "Luck—"

Peabody lifted a hand in a farewell salute, and motioned to the men with him to dismount. "Obliged—and the same to you. Sure thank you for showing us where the Hurleys was holed up."

"Was the least I could do," Dan said and rode off down the trail.

He'd go into town, he guessed, see about getting himself a meal—if there was a restaurant in the settlement—and then sit down and do some serious thinking about the future.

He reckoned he was standing at a crossroads, and the decision of which direction to take was going to be mighty important; was it to be J. J. Hamilton's ranch in Wyoming, or the Wakefield spread and all the promising advantages that went with it? Working for women—for Cameo Wakefield, actually, would—

"No—Peabody—wait!"

The piercing voice of a woman, followed by a scream of terror, and then the quick, sudden rattle of gunshots brought Ragan to a stop.

Peabody and his men had evidently closed in on Sutton and the others—but why the shooting? The outlaws, unsuspecting, could hardly have put up a fight. Curious, disturbed, Ragan swung the sorrel about and headed back up the trail at a gallop.

16

Dan reached the edge of the clearing and drew to a stop. A coldness swept him, hardening his jaw. Sutton, Greer, Swinnerton, and May Hurley lay dead in front of the shack. Apparently they had come out into the open and walked directly into the waiting guns of Peabody and his deputies.

Dismounting, anger stirring through him, Ragan strode deeper into the yard. Peabody and the others were standing near the doorway to the cabin with their backs to him, examining the contents of the black saddlebags.

"I reckon it's all here," he heard the big man say as he drew close.

At that moment Dave Kitchens heard the crunch of Dan's boots, and pistol still in hand, he whirled.

"You damn fool!" Kitchens shouted, recognizing Ragan. "Don't you know no better'n to sneak up on a man like that?"

Dan's smile was bitter. "Wasn't sneaking up. You're just a mite jumpy—and I can see why," he said, looking around at the sprawled bodies of the outlaws. Only Greer and Swinnerton had managed to draw their weapons. "You had them cold—why'd you shoot them down like—"

"Done what we had to," Peabody broke in curtly, hanging the Mexican saddlebags over his thick shoulder and moving up to Ragan. "Ain't always easy to just collar a man. Sutton and his kind usually puts up a fight."

"Sutton's not even holding his gun. Neither is the woman—"

"Outlaws—killers. A man don't take no chance when he's dealing with them—'specially when you're after them for robbery."

"And murder," Rufe Cobb said. "Don't be forgetting that."

"Yeh, murder, too," Peabody agreed.

Ragan shook his head. "Still looks like a cold-blooded killing to me, outlaws or not. And the woman—"

"You been told before she was plenty bad

146

as any man you ever come across—worse in fact than most," Peabody snapped, temper raising his voice. "If she'd had a gun—"

"She didn't. And the others there—Sutton hadn't even pulled his and looks like Greer and Swinnerton had barely cleared leather with their iron when you opened up on them."

"Tough on them," Arlie Redd said dryly. "Just turned out we was faster—"

"I don't see as it makes any difference anyway," Peabody said. "They was all no-accounts—outlaws. They got just what they had coming—and usually get. Their kind never dies of old age."

"Maybe, but the way I savvy the law, they had a trial coming," Dan said stubbornly. "It's supposed to be up to a judge what's to happen to them. I sure doubt he'd sentence the woman to die."

"They'd a lived to have a trial, if they'd wanted. But no, they tried to shoot it out with us and just didn't make it," Peabody said with a ring of finality in his voice. He turned to Cobb. "Rufe, you and the boys tote the bodies into the house and lay them on the bed or whatever's handy. We'll stop by the marshal's office when we go by town, tell him what happened and have him send somebody out to take care of things.''

Cobb and the other deputies turned away and together began to move the dead outlaws into the cabin. Ragan stood in silence, watching for a time, disapproval strong on his features. After a bit, feeling Ed Peabody's steady gaze on him, he glanced up.

''I take it you ain't liking what we—I had to do here—''

Dan shook his head. ''Don't seem to me it was needful. I figure you could have easy taken them in—not shot them down like a bunch of mad dogs. Hell, Sheriff, you had the drop on them!''

Peabody swore angrily. ''There's a devil of a lot you've got to learn about outlaws, cowboy! And you sure ain't making me happy standing there telling me how I ought to do my job when—''

The big lawman broke off. The bodies had been carried into the cabin, and Kitchens, followed by Redd and Rufe Cobb, was reappearing.

''But it don't make a tinker's damn to me,'' he continued, motioning at Cobb to close the door. ''I do what I figure I ought. Now, suppose you climb back up on your horse and move out. I don't want to hear no

148

more of your lip."

"Yeh," Rufe Cobb said, dropping a hand onto the butt of the his pistol threateningly. "Best you do what Ed says or you'll answer up to interfering with the law!"

Dan Ragan shrugged. Wheeling slowly, he started for the sorrel. Peabody knew best how to handle outlaws, he reckoned, and he supposed there were times when the law was forced to deal harshly with them—just as he and his men had done here. Maybe it didn't seem fair and right to shoot them all down, but then Sutton and the others had chosen to live outside the law and therefore were not deserving of any consideration.

Reaching the sorrel, he jerked the lines free of the oak brush into which he had looped them and went to the saddle. Looking back he saw Peabody, flanked by his men in the center of the yard, watching him narrowly. Raising his hand coolly, Ragan touched the brim of his hat. None of the four responded. Ragan grinned. He guessed he'd rubbed them all the wrong way, questioning their actions as he had.

No matter. He held no kindly thoughts for the outlaws, but he still believed that Peabody and his men killing—murdering, actually—Sutton and his partners as they had, was not necessary. Furthermore, he'd always think so. But it was over, finished, and nothing could be done about it.

Ragan glanced to the west. The sun was not far from setting and there was no point in continuing on his way, whichever direction it would be, until morning. He'd go on into Blackwater just as he'd planned earlier, get himself a meal, a couple of drinks, and put up at the hotel—if there was one—for the night. He'd have a chance to sort out his thoughts now that he had nothing else on his mind, and make his decision.

It was a good five miles to the town. It proved to be a general store, a couple of saloons, a feed and seed supply house, a livery stable and several run-down residences. There was no sign of a lawman's office, Dan noted absently; he reckoned Peabody would have to make other arrangements for handling the dead outlaws.

Everything was locked up with the exception of one saloon, and pausing there, he ordered a drink. One shot of the raw redeye was sufficient for Ragan, and since nothing else was open for business, he doubled back to the gelding in the now full darkness and made his way through the trees and brush to the lake that lay nearby. He could make a fairly comfortable camp there, both water and grass being readily available to the sorrel, and he had enough grub in his sack to satisfy his own needs.

He arrived at the lake a short time later, rode along its edge, listening idly to the croaking of frogs until he found a suitable place and halted. Unsaddling the sorrel and removing the bridle, Dan staked the big horse out a few yards below the spot he'd chosen as a camp site, and then set about making himself comfortable.

An hour or so later, with coffee boiling over a low fire and a mixture of dried meat, onions, and beans—cooked days earlier and carried in a fruit jar for just such moments—stewing in a skillet beside it, Ragan began to feel at ease.

It had been a long, hard day, a long hard week, he thought, setting the stew off the flames to cool and then pouring himself a cup of the coffee. It had never occurred to him that he might become involved in all that had taken place—the Hurleys, the Wakefields, Ed Peabody and the law, but he had. Thankfully, that was all behind him now.

Except for the Wakefields. He still had to make up his mind to accept the job they had offered, or not—and the time to do so was now, this very night. The day when it would be too late to sign on with J. J. Hamilton in Wyoming was drawing close, and he must either—

"Just set easy," a voice warned from the darkness beyond the flare of the fire. "There's three guns pointing straight at you. Make a wrong move and you're dead! This is the law talking!"

17

The law again! Damn it to hell's fire! Dan Ragan swore deeply, angrily. He'd already run up against a party of fakes and one bunch that was genuine—and yet here was another throwing down on him!

"All right, all right!" he answered in frustration. "Come on in. I won't give you no trouble—but you're too damn late!"

Three men, appearing at different points, emerged from the shadows and moved into the firelight. Each held a pistol—and each wore a star that glittered in the light of the flickering flames.

"Name's Avery—Sam Avery," the one in the center announced.

He was small and lean, with sharp, narrowed eyes and a straight line for a mouth. Dressed in tall, wide-brimmed hat, stovepipe boots, cord pants, gray shirt and vest, he looked as if he'd been in the saddle for days. His star bore the single graven word in black—SHERIFF.

"Who're you?" he demanded brusquely.

"Dan Ragan—"

"Fair enough, Ragan—let's do some talking. I'm the sheriff from over in Texas—Sacksville. These two men are deputies—Ned Linder and Jud Hartman. Now tell me what you meant when you said we're too late."

"You hunting the Hurley gang—the bunch that killed and robbed some trail boss?"

"That we are," Avery replied, nodding. "What do you know about them?"

"Another posse's already taken over."

Avery glanced at his deputies in surprise. "How do you know?"

"Was me that showed them where the Hurley gang was holed up—a house a few miles from here."

Sam Avery holstered his weapon. Pulling off his hat he ran his fingers through his hair wearily.

"Didn't know there was anybody else trailing them," he said. "Seems we been pounding our butts in the saddle for nothing. You know who the lawmen were?" he

154

added to Ragan.

Dan motioned at the can of coffee setting off the fire and being eyed hungrily by both Linder and Hartman. "Help yourselves. . . . Yeh, I know. Names were Peabody—Ed Peabody. And Rufe Cobb, Dave Kitchens, and Arlie Redd."

A sudden hush had fallen over the three men. Sam Avery was staring at Dan, and his deputies had paused, Linder with the can of coffee in his hand, the other with the tin cup Ragan had been using, their fixed attention also on him.

"Who?" the sheriff said in a taut voice.

Ragan repeated the names. A vague, disturbing suspicion began to lift within him when he saw the reaction his words had on the men.

"Something wrong?"

"Wrong!" Avery repeated heavily. "Ed Peabody ain't no lawman and them that was with him ain't either. Friend, you done one of the worst bunches of outlaws in West Texas a good turn when you handed that money over to them!"

Dan got slowly to his feet, swearing raggedly. Again he'd been made a fool of—played for a sucker! Shrugging wearily, he looked out over the lake, a silver mirror now in the moonlight. The pulsing buzz of cicadas and chirp of crickets was now all but overcoming the sporadic croaking of the frogs.

"Well, I reckon that's that." Avery said resignedly, reaching out to Linder for the can of coffee and taking a deep swallow when he had it in hand. "How'd you happen to know where Ab Hurley and his bunch were?"

"Hurley's dead," Ragan said in a voice filled with disgust, and then related the circumstances of how he came into possession of the money and managed to deliver it to Hurley's wife.

"Some friends of his—man named Sutton, another'n called Cully Greer, and a third named Swinnerton, stopped me at the edge of town. Said they were lawmen, along with being Hurley's friends, and were about to ride out looking for him."

"Why?"

Ragan shook his head. Repeating again the details of the incident which pointed up his own gullibility was a tortuous process, but the facts were necessary and he laid them out one by one regardless of the pain and shamed personal pride.

"The way Peabody told it, they were with Hurley when that drover got killed and

156

robbed. They split up when Peabody and his bunch moved in on them and were to meet here where Hurley's wife was waiting.''

"May—that her name?''

"That's what she was called. You know her?''

Avery turned his head, spat into the brush. "Hell, ain't a lawman in West Texas or Eastern New Mexico who don't know May Hurley—or Ab either. Comes down to it, she was always the brains of the outfit. They turn the money over to Peabody and them without a scrap?''

"Wasn't there,'' Ragan explained. "Took them to the house where the Hurleys were living, then rode on.'' Dan hesitated, remembering how Ed Peabody—or was it one of the others?—had warned him to move out, not to take the chance of getting hit by a stray bullet. And then later, when he had questioned the killing of the Sutton bunch, they had made it clear he'd best be on his way.

"You was mighty dang lucky they didn't shoot you full of holes to keep you quiet,'' Hartman said, nursing his coffee. "Peabody ain't what you'd call soft-hearted.''

"Seemed to enjoy acting like a lawman, and being treated like one. Knew I was on my way to take a job, too, and probably figured I'd soon be out of the way."

Avery was studying Ragan closely. "Then you ain't for sure that Peabody's got the money. You took him and his bunch there, then left."

"He got it all right," Dan said. "Was down the trail a piece when I heard a woman—was May Hurley—yell, and then there was gunshots. Her yelling made me sort of curious, so I doubled back to the shack. She was laying dead in the yard. So were Sutton, Greer, and Swinnerton. Peabody and the others were counting the money.

"From what I could tell by looking, Sutton and them didn't get the chance to put up a fight—or even throw down their guns and quit. They just got shot down."

Avery smiled grimly. "Expect by then you knew they weren't lawmen—that you'd made a hell of a mistake."

"Seeing all those bodies and how they got killed hit me plenty hard, all right, and I started asking why it had to be like that. Peabody said it was the only way they could do it—that Sutton and them were mighty dangerous and that they put up a fight.

"Sutton and May Hurley didn't have a

gun in their hands, and it looked to me like the other two men drew but never got a chance to shoot. Pointed that out to Peabody and it riled him some. Claimed lawmen sometimes had to handle things that way—and then I got told again to move on—was threatened, in fact."

Ned Linder put the now empty coffee can back on the ground near the fire. The flames were lowering and he absently picked up a handful of the sticks Dan had gathered and dropped them into the flames. As the fire blazed brightly, he shrugged.

"Doing what you done, mister, is sure going to cause a lot of misery. That money belonged to a whole bunch of people—thirty families, in fact, all small ranchers. They'd pooled their herds and turned them over to Jim Drayson to drive to market and sell. He done just that and was on his way back with the cash when Hurley and his gang bushwhacked him and Otto Coogan, who was siding him. Killed them both."

"Didn't know there was two men killed," Dan said, and then added: "Seems like a hell of a lot of cash for a man to be packing."

"Jim had to pay off each one of them ranchers as he rode in and had to have cash money. Wasn't scared of losing it, I reckon.

Was only a short ride from the depot in Sacksville to the ranches—and he had Coogan sort of riding shotgun with him."

Hartman had drawn a blackened briar pipe from the pocket of his coat and was tamping its charred bowl full with shreds of tobacco. "Expect them folks'll all live through it," he said without looking up, "but it'll sure bust most of them. They would've been figuring on the cash to see them through the next couple of years."

"Tough all right," Avery agreed. "Shame, too. Folks that works hard as they do deserve better."

Ragan was silent for a long minute as he gave the lawmen's words deep thought. Then, "Hurley's shack's about five miles from here. Can take you there right now if you want."

Avery shook his head. "Not much use. Peabody and his bunch are long gone by now." He paused, looking up into the star-filled sky, listening to the sounds of the night. "Nope," he said in a final sort of way, "I'm calling it quits right here. I'm out of my jurisdiction for one thing, and there ain't no way of telling which way that bunch went."

Jud Hartman blew a cloud of savory pipe

smoke into the still air. "Likely done divvied up the cash and split—all going different directions."

"Likely," Avery agreed. "Time we was getting back to Sacksville, too. We've been gone quite a spell and Hartman and Linder've both got regular jobs to look after—they just volunteered to side me. Jim Drayson was a friend of theirs."

"That mean you're just forgetting it—just letting Peabody and his bunch ride off with the money?"

"Nothing else I can do—"

"And there's the killing of May Hurley and Sutton and the others. They'll be getting away with their murders."

"Nothing to bawl over there," Ned Linder said. "Would be a mighty big help to folks if the outlaws would all turn on each other and kill themselves off."

"I figure I've done all that can be expected of me," Sam Avery continued. "We tracked them far as we could, and we know now who has the money. I aim to go back to my office and get out wanted dodgers on Ed Peabody and his crowd quick as I can to every town in this part of the country."

"That'll nail them sooner than we could if we try to pick up their trails and start hunting them," Hartman said. "You want to head back tonight, Sam? My horse is good for a couple more hours."

"Yeh, let's start back," the lawman said. He turned to Dan. "Obliged to you for your help. Telling us what you did saved us plenty of time. Expect you'll be moving on come morning, to take that job you're after. Want to wish you good luck—and forget all about this. Was a deal you got rooked into and couldn't help."

Ragan stirred impatiently. "I was a damn fool to trust any of that bunch—"

Avery smiled kindly. "Now, don't go blaming yourself too much. Biggest fool I can think of is a man who won't trust anybody. The law'll run that bunch down."

Ragan stood grimly silent in the glow of the fire. He was thinking of the trouble—of the misery, as Ned Linder had put it—that his actions were going to bring to the people who had bet their futures on the money they expected to receive from selling their cattle. It was his fault, indirectly and inadvertently to be sure, but his nevertheless.

"Just you forget about it," Sam Avery said again, motioning Linder and Hartman toward the horses, and moving in behind them. "Just leave it up to the law to take care of them."

Dan Ragan's features were hard set, his eyes all but closed. "Not the way I see it, Sheriff," he said. "I've got a law of my own. I cause somebody grief—I make it right for them."

Avery paused. "That your way of saying you're going after them?"

"What I figure to do. I was wrong right from the start—thinking Ab Hurley was on the square—and then swallowing what Sutton and Peabody told me—taking their word that they were lawmen. Those ranchers and their families will suffer on account of me. Maybe some of them will have to give up and quit—and I sure couldn't stand having that on my conscience. I'll track down those outlaws and get that money back if it takes me the rest of my life."

An expression of doubt crossed Avery's lined face. "That'll be a mighty big job that you maybe better leave to the law."

Ragan shook his head. "No, it's up to me and nobody else."

The lawman came fully around, took a step toward Dan and extended his hand. There was a sort of pride showing in his eyes now which overrode the doubt.

"It's a pleasure to know you, son," he

said. "Take care, and good luck." Then he followed his deputies into the darkness beyond the fire's light.

18

Ragan pivoted slowly, eyes on the again dwindling fire. His mind was set and his determination to find Ed Peabody and the other outlaws and right the wrong he had furthered, if not committed, was growing stronger with each passing minute.

And he'd not wait—he'd start immediately. Maybe the outlaws were still at Hurley's cabin; maybe they had decided to wait until morning before moving out. It was a slim hope but Dan Ragan knew that he must be certain of it, that he had to know one way or the other. Time was of ultimate importance now, and the sooner he got on the outlaws' trail, the sooner he would bring them to account.

Squatting, he took up the spider and tossed the remainder of its contents into the nearby brush for the benefit of any varmint seeking food. Emptying the grounds from the coffee can, he collected it, the skillet, tin cup, and spoon he had been using and hurriedly moving to the edge of the lake, gave them a hasty washing. Returning to camp, Dan restored them and his sack of grub to their places on his saddle, and then carried the hull to where the sorrel was grazing.

He'd go first to Hurley's cabin. If, as he feared, the outlaws had already pulled out, he'd cut back to the town and ask if anyone there had seen them riding off. If he turned up no answers, that would tell him which direction the outlaws had taken; he'd have no choice but to return to the shack and search about for tracks.

The sorrel ready, and having refilled his canteen with fresh water from the lake, Ragan mounted and doubled back through the brush to the trail. He didn't push the big gelding hard, realizing the horse had enjoyed only a minimum amount of rest, but permitted him to pick his way along the path, fairly easy to follow in the strong moonlight.

A half mile or so short of the clearing where the Hurley cabin stood a frown crossed

Dan's face. The faint odor of smoke had reached him—and grew stronger as he drew nearer. It could be a campfire, he reasoned, and if so, it meant the outlaws were still there. But the smoke didn't have the good, clean smell of a campfire; instead it was tainted, bearing the pungent odor of burned cloth—and flesh.

The realization of what that could mean swept through Ragan, and no longer leaving the pace up to the sorrel, he spurred the horse into a fast lope, keeping to the softer shoulder of the trail where the sound of hoofs would be muffled.

Approaching the edge of the clearing, Dan pulled off into the shadows, dismounted, and tethered the sorrel to a small tree. Then, pistol in hand, he worked his way forward to the fringe of brush that surrounded the house. Abruptly Dan Ragan came to a halt. All that remained of the shack was a blackened square of smoking, smoldering ashes.

Grim, Ragan circled the ruin, staying within the bordering brush while he searched for signs of the outlaws. He found no indication of their presence, and concluding they had already pulled out, he stepped into the open and crossed to what was left of the house.

There was little that indicated the house had once been inhabited—the iron framework of a stove, a few tin cans, bits of wire, and other metal all blackened and twisted by the intense heat that had engulfed them.

It was as he feared. The bodies of the Hurley woman, Sutton, Cully Greer, and Bob Swinnerton were there among the ashes too. He could see a skull, partly visible in the debris, along with other bits of evidence. Ed Peabody and his gang had taken care to hide the murders they had committed. Anyone chancing upon the scene and finding the remains of several persons in the charred wreckage of the house would simply assume there had been a tragic accident.

Only he—and the outlaws—knew better, Dan realized, turning away and walking slowly to his horse. But in that the advantage was his; they were unaware that he knew.

It was too dark to look for tracks, despite the light from the stars and moon. He'd best follow his original plan to go to Blackwater and make inquiries, and then if he failed to turn up any information, return to the shack—or what had been a shack. Swinging up into the saddle, he pointed the sorrel west, wondering as he did what had happened to the horses that Sutton and his friends were riding. No doubt they had either been freed by the Peabody gang or, frightened by the fire, had managed to pull loose from the hitch rack where he had last seen them. Whatever, they would do all right in the area until someone claimed them.

The town was dark when Ragan, after tarrying at the edge of the lake for an hour or so while he awaited first light, rode into the settlement's lone street and moved along the fronts of the various business buildings. Halting at the rack of the saloon he had earlier patronized, he considered pounding on the door of the place to rouse the proprietor and inquire whether the outlaws had been there or not.

It was necessary, he felt, to get on their trail as quickly as possible and would justify his actions. Dropping from the saddle, he looped the reins over the cross bar of the rack, and stepping up onto the landing knocked vigorously on the wooden door.

There was no response to that effort and he tried again, this time hammering much harder with a clenched fist. At once a light somewhere deep inside the structure showed faintly against a window shade, and then, shortly, the door swung inward and the saloonman, lamp held above his head, peered out.

"What the hell are you wanting this time of the night?" he demanded sourly. "I'm closed up—"

"Know that," Ragan replied, "but this is mighty important. Did you have four strangers in here some time after the middle of the afternoon? One was a big man—"

"They was here. What about it?"

Ragan's hopes lifted. "Which way did they go when they rode out?"

"Wouldn't know. Come in about dark. Had a couple of drinks—bought a bottle apiece, and left. Never paid no mind to which way they was going."

Ragan drew back, disappointed. But he'd not give up yet; he'd ask others in the settlement. Surely someone, in a town as small and quiet as Blackwater, would have noticed four strangers passing through. One thing, there was no point now in returning to the ruins of the cabin and searching for hoof prints leading from the clearing. They would end up in the town—and he already knew the outlaws had gone there.

"Why don't you go talk to Henry Gholson?" Dan heard the saloon owner say. "Runs the livery stable down the street. If anybody seen your friends leaving it'd been him."

Ragan nodded. "Not my friends—but I'm obliged to you. And I sure hate it if I woke you up, but catching up with that bunch is mighty important to me."

The saloonman lowered his lamp and stepped back. "It's all right—sort of used to it. There's always some fool coming along pounding on the door asking directions or something," he said in a grumbling voice as he closed the heavy panel.

Ragan returned to the sorrel and, mounting, hurried off down the quiet street for the square, slanted roof building that housed the stable. There was no light visible but the wide, sliding door was half open, and turning into it, Dan halted in the runway and looked about.

In the musty gloom he located a door to his left, and assuming it to be Gholson's quarters, dismounted and stepped up to it. He rapped sharply and got a quick response.

"Coming! Keep your shirt on!"

Dan fell back a stride to wait. The door opened, and a man in undershirt and overalls, holding a lantern in his hand, faced him from a circle of white whiskers and hair.

"You want to put up your animal?"

"Can't spare the time for that," Dan replied, "but I can sure use a bag of oats to take with me—and some information."

Gholson said, "Sure," in a cheerful sort of voice and, ignoring his bare feet, came on out into the runway. "I'll fix you up a little sack—about a quarter's worth."

"Be fine," Ragan said, trailing the old man to a room a bit farther down where he evidently had feed stored. The sorrel, left unattended, and smelling fresh hay in a nearby stall, had moved off on his own and was helping himself at the manger.

"Looking for four men," Ragan said as the stableman, hanging the lantern on a nail, reached for an old flour sack and began to cup oats into it. "Big fellow on a gray. Others were riding blacks and a bay. Were in Hoseman's saloon about dark, I was told. I'm trying to find out which way they headed when they left here."

"East," Gholson said promptly, lifting the bag and gauging the weight of its contents. "Took the road for Kansas."

Ragan sighed with relief. He hadn't expected it to be so easy, so simple, but then he realized the outlaws were not expecting anyone to be on their trail and thus took no pains to cover up their movements. To their way of thinking, they had gotten away clear.

"I reckon that's about a quarter's worth," Gholson said, closing the sack and tying a string around the neck. "That what you wanted to know about them fellows?"

"Sure is," Ragan answered, "and I'm obliged to you." Reaching into his pocket he dug out a silver dollar. "Horse of mine's made himself right at home in that front stall. This ought to cover the oats, the hay he's eating, and me rousting you out of bed."

Gholson grinned, accepting the coin. "Does—for a fact. You taking off right now after them fellows?"

"Right now," Ragan said, and backing the sorrel out of the stall, he stepped up into the saddle. "Came past a shack about five miles east of here. There'd been a fire. Expect somebody ought to go out and look into it."

"Five miles east?" Gholson murmured. "That'd be the old Burwinkle place. Been some folks just move in there."

"Nothing but ashes now," Dan said. Then, "The road to Kansas—where do I find it?"

"Just turn left when you go out my door.

173

Road forks up the ways apiece. Take the right hand."

Dan nodded. "Obliged," he said and put the sorrel, still munching at a mouthful of hay, into motion.

19

Dan Ragan had given no thought at all to his own affairs, to the fact that setting out to overtake the outlaws and recover the money from them could cause him to lose out on both the Wyoming and Wakefield Ranch foreman jobs. He had simply dismissed both from his mind, the sense of obligation to the thirty or so Texas ranchers whom he did not even know now foremost in his consideration.

A straightforward, uncomplicated sort of man, Ragan took things as they came, one by one, and handled them as best he could regardless of personal cost and consequence. That he was not disturbed about his future was usual. If he lost out—well, that's the way the cards fell sometimes. He'd just have to hunt himself up a job somewhere else when he was finished with his present undertaking.

That could be a fair-sized chore. Ranch hands weren't exactly in short supply, although good, experienced ones usually found work somewhere. And too, Harvey Brazil had told him that maybe there'd be a place for him if things didn't work out in Wyoming—but that was only a maybe.

The morning wore on as the mesa country about him girded itself for the day's strong heat. Already the red-faced bluffs were beginning to lose their deep color and assume a faded look. Most of the wild flowers— bright yellow marigolds, purple sand verbenas, milk vetch, white locoweed, and others, having trapped their quota of the night's dew, had closed and were folded limply forward to await the cooler hours coming later in the day. But the stout yuccas, the ones the Indians called *Yaybi-tsa-si*, the thistles, prickly pear, and grotesque cholla cactuses standing aloof and distinct from their neighbors, defied the rising temperatures.

Far off to his right in a broad swale, Dan could see a grove of bright, green-leafed cottonwoods, and along the sometimes wide and shallow and other times deep and

narrow arroyos down which occasional
torrents of muddy water raced, Apache
Plume, uteberry, sage, and other brushy
shrubs grew thick on their banks. Small,
globular cedar trees, their foliage a deep
green, were to be occasionally seen
silhouetted against the prairie-grass-covered
slopes while overhead a steel-blue sky bent
over all.

It was new country to Dan Ragan, and he
took note of it as the sorrel loped steadily
along the well-defined road; likely he would
have taken much enjoyment from what he
saw had his purpose for being there not been
of such a grim nature.

Late in the morning, smoke curling up
against the horizon to the north drew his
attention. It proved to be from a homestead,
and since the house with its collection of
ragtag outbuildings lay but a short distance
off the trail, Dan veered from course and
rode into the littered yard fronting the wood-
and-soddy structure.

At once a worn-looking woman with
several small children clustered about her
came through the doorway and, hand
shading her eyes from the sun, faced him.

"What're you wanting?" she demanded
suspiciously.

Ragan looked beyond her to a field where a man, evidently her husband, was working the ground. The place appeared dry, wind-scoured, and starved. Farming, Dan reckoned, was no better a bet in this area than it was down in the Axhead country. Beef was the only successful crop, but newcomers, always optimistic, could never believe it.

"Nothing, missus," Ragan said, "except I'd like to ask about some men I'm trying to catch up with. Was four of them—one riding a gray—"

"Was by here last evening—late," the woman said, reaching down to disengage the fingers of one of the smaller children dragging at her faded skirt. "Was wanting to eat. We didn't have nothing much so they went on. Done their eating at the way station, I expect."

Ragan's interest stirred. "Way station?"

"About ten mile up the road. Can get yourself most anything you'd be wanting there—eats and drinks and card playing, and the like."

Dan expressed his thanks to the woman and returned to the road. His hopes had risen once more; if his luck was running good he'd find Peabody and the others at this way station. With plenty of cash and no reason to fear a pursuit, they could be celebrating their newly acquired wealth.

It was more than just a way station, Ragan saw as he headed into what looked to be a small settlement. It evidently had no name, as none was apparent on the half-dozen buildings—all saloons offering liquor, gambling, and women—standing off to either side of the stagecoach stop.

Pulling up to the long hitch rack at the side of the principal saloon, the Cactus Rose, Ragan sat for a time looking over the horses waiting hipshot in the hot sun. Bays were plentiful, as were blacks. There were a few other shades—sorrels, chestnuts, a paint or two, several whites—but no grays. Apparently Peabody was not at the Cactus Rose, and that fact seemed to indicate that Cobb, Redd, and Kitchens were not there either. Raising his glance, Dan looked beyond the saloon to the other racks visible. There were horses there, too, but no grays.

Heaving a sigh, Ragan came off the saddle and secured the gelding. It was near noon; he'd get himself a bit of dinner, ask a few questions about the men he was trailing, and then move on. It seemed unlikely that they could have passed up the way station; halting there even for a brief time, they could have left some clue as to their destination.

Crossing the broad landing, he entered the Cactus Rose through its open doorway. A dozen or more men were at the bar, a like number scattered about at the tables playing poker, chuck-a-luck, and bucking the tiger. Women, gaudily dressed and with heavily rouged and powdered faces, were numerous. A stairway off the back of the large, rectangular room led to a second floor at the rear of the place. The room was noisy with voices and heavy with smoke and the smell of liquor.

Patiently Ragan scanned the faces in the saloon, saw none that were familiar, and moved up to the long bar, a crude but efficient counter with a narrow strip of board nailed to its edge that prevented glasses from sliding off and falling to the floor. On the wall behind it were shelves all well filled with bottles and extra glasses. There was no mirror, Dan saw, and reckoned that was much too expensive a fixture to risk.

"Whiskey," he ordered as the bartender paused before him. There were no facilities for eating, he noticed.

"Two bits," the bartender said when he had poured the drink.

Ragan dropped a quarter on the counter and took the shot glass between a thumb and forefinger. "Was hoping to get a bite to eat in here but looks like I can't. Where does a man go when he gets hungry?"

"Over at the station—the stage depot," the barkeep said. "We don't serve grub and they don't sell liquor."

Dan nodded, tipped the glass to his lips, and downed the whiskey. Suddenly he came to attention. Descending the stairs were Dave Kitchens and Arlie Redd, each with a woman at his side. They were laughing and talking, and apparently having completed their business in one of the upstairs rooms, were now on their way to the bar.

Taut, cool, Ragan set his empty glass on the counter. Reaching down he grasped the butt of the pistol on his hip, lifted the weapon slightly, and let it settle back loosely in the holster, thus assuring himself that it was not only there but ready. Then, movements deliberate and devoid of any wasted effort, he stepped away from the bar and moved toward the stairs. Midway he came to a stop.

"Redd—Kitchens! I've come for the money you took!"

The two men froze as the saloon plunged

instantly into silence. The woman at Arlie Redd's side jerked away from him, hurrying back up the steps to get clear of any possible gunfire. The one with Kitchens chose an opposite course—coming on down the stairs and disappearing into the crowd.

"I don't want no trouble in here, mister," Ragan heard the bartender say. He shook his head.

"Up to them. They can fork over the money they took or they can go for their guns. Makes no damn difference to me."

Kitchens had remained motionless, his face sullen, his mouth tight-lipped. He stared at Dan unblinkingly. Finally he shrugged.

"I told Ed we should've put a bullet in you," he said. He grabbed for his pistol.

Ragan's draw was smooth, double fast. He fired almost before Kitchens had his weapon out. The impact of the heavy slug, at such close range, drove the outlaw back against the stair's railing. He buckled, rebounded, and then pitched forward, head first, down the steps.

Ragan swung his attention through the swirling smoke to Arlie Redd. The outlaw was racing up the stairs two at a time. He reached the top just as Dan brought his weapon to bear, seized the woman who had been with him only moments before, and shoved her at Ragan.

Dan swore as he tried to get a line on the outlaw now disappearing into the dark hallway that separated the two rows of rooms and led on to the rear of the building. The impulse to follow Redd—either go after him down the corridor, or leave the saloon by its front entrance, circle the building and cut him off—came to Ragan. No, it was better to hunt him down later—he did have Dave Kitchens.

Turning slowly, Dan scoured the faces before him with a hard, steady look. "This man will have maybe seventy-five hundred dollars on him. It's stolen money. Same goes for his partner. I've come after it and I'm taking it off him now. If any of you wants to argue about it, let's start now."

There was no response. Ragan, holstering his gun, stepped to where Kitchens lay, half on the floor, half on the lower steps. Reaching down, Dan caught the outlaw by the collar and dragged him the remainder of the way off the stairs. Turning him onto his back, Ragan began to search his pockets.

A grunt of satisfaction came from Dan's lips as his fingers came in contact with a large roll of bills and an amount of silver.

Ignoring the coins, he glanced briefly at the currency, concluding that there should be more. A slight bulge around Kitchens' waist caught his attention. He jerked the blood-stained shirt aside. The outlaw was wearing a new money belt.

Releasing the buckle's tongue, Ragan pulled it free. Now satisfied, he drew himself fully upright and, crossing to the bartender, laid the roll of bills and the belt on the counter.

"Count this out for me," he said brusquely, and moving toward the door, he added: "I aim to be right back."

20

Gaining the saloon's landing in half-a-dozen long strides, Ragan cut right and circled the building at a run. Reaching the back corner, he halted. Redd could be waiting for him.

But there was no sign of the outlaw on the upper stair level, on the steps, or anywhere close by on the ground below. Dan, cautious, moved farther into the open, his glance probing the rear of the buildings adjacent. Redd was nowhere in sight. Wheeling, Ragan crossed to a man working on a red-wheeled buggy a dozen yards farther on.

"You see somebody come out the upstairs back door of the saloon in the last few minutes?"

The workman—young, dressed in overalls, undershirt, heavy shoes, and a ragged straw hat, raised his head. "No, ain't nobody come out or gone in the Cactus since I've been here—and that's most of a hour."

"You sure of that?"

The man straightened and his eyes sparked. "Said it, didn't I?" he demanded peevishly. "I ain't seen nobody 'cepting real early—"

Ragan had turned, doubling back to the street fronting the saloon. If what the workman said could be relied on, and Dan had no reason to doubt him, Redd was still inside the Cactus Rose.

Reaching the door, Ragan hurriedly stepped inside and moved to the bar. The man behind the counter was busy counting the money that had been handed him. Piles of paper and a few gold eagles were neatly arranged before him while a dozen by-standers looked on, fascinated by the array of wealth. He looked up as Dan halted at the bar.

"Ain't done yet. Hell of a lot of money—"

"Redd—Kitchens' partner," Ragan cut in. "He come down the stairs while I was outside?"

The bartender shook his head. Dan glanced about at the bystanders. They nodded, verifying the saloonman's statement.

"There any way out of the upstairs except by that back door?"

Again his answer was a shake of the head. That could mean only one thing; Arlie Redd was hiding in one of the rooms on the second floor.

"You figure to kill him, too—like you done that fellow laying there?" one of the onlookers asked.

"I mean to get back the money he took," Ragan replied evenly. "It's up to him how I have to do it."

"Shame—sure seems like a real fine man. Generous, and young, too. You for certain he's got your money?"

Ragan was already moving toward the stairs, his pistol in hand and ready. "I'm sure," he murmured as he started to ascend the steps.

He'd best take it slow and careful, he realized. Redd could be hiding anywhere in the shadowy area of the saloon's second floor. And once he'd gained that level, it would be smart to keep an eye on the door that would be at the end of the hall. The outlaw, seeing or hearing him on that upper floor, might try to escape by that route.

Ragan reached the top of the stairs, found himself in a sort of gallery off which the hallway ran at right angles. Studying the corridor, he saw there were three doors on each side which would indicate a like number of rooms. As there were no other doors it was logical to assume Redd would be found in one of those.

Backing to the rail of the gallery, Ragan threw his glance to the saloon below. The bartender had finished his counting and, arms folded, was standing by awaiting further developments. The patrons also were quiet, making only soft shuffling noises when they stirred about and speaking with low voices as they, too, waited to see how matters would turn out.

But Dan's narrowed, searching eyes had no interest in them; he was making certain that Arlie Redd had not managed somehow to leave the upper floor of the Cactus Rose, slip by unnoticed, and reach his horse.

Ragan drew up sharply as that thought came to him. Reach his horse—that's what Redd would attempt to do! Frowning, Dan squared his bearings. The hitch rack was on the south side of the saloon. Chances were the outlaw would be hiding in a room on that same side of the building, holding back until he felt it was safe to climb through a window, drop to the ground, and make it to his horse.

Dan immediately crossed to the first door on the left wall of the hall. Grasping the knob, he twisted. Then, drawing back from the frame to avoid placing himself in the line of fire, he flung the door open.

The room—hot and stuffy, smelling of sweat and liquor—was empty. Dan, stooping to see under the bed, and finding nothing, hurriedly moved to the window and raised it. The hitch rack with its dozen or so horses was almost directly below. A bay he thought might be the outlaw's was one of those present, but he could not be sure.

Wheeling, Dan returned to the hall and walked quickly to the entrance of the room next in line. Following the same procedure as earlier, he again drew a blank. Ragan's jaw hardened. Had Redd outsmarted him? It didn't seem likely. He had the man trapped inside the saloon; he had to be there somewhere.

Walking swiftly and quietly on to the last door on that side of the hall, Ragan grasped the knob. This could be it—this could be where the outlaw was hiding if he had planned to escape by a window and get to his horse.

Tensing, pistol ready, Dan threw back the door and jerked aside. There was no reaction, no sound—only the blast of trapped, heated air laden with the smells he had encountered when entering the other rooms. Cursing softly, puzzled, Ragan moved through the doorway and started to cross to the window for his look at the horses below. Nothing had changed. The same animals were still there dozing in the hot sunlight.

Suddenly he heard a quick rush of booted feet in the corridor behind him. Dan whirled, getting a brief glimpse of a woman in a yellow dress as she jerked the door closed. Lunging forward Dan grasped the knob and pulled. The door gave only inches. The woman was hanging tight from the opposite side.

"Get the hell away from there or I'll shoot!" Ragan yelled, and put his weight into a second try.

The door gave abruptly. Ragan, off balance, stumbled backward, caught himself—and then went down full length as the woman flung herself upon him.

Oaths ripping from his lips, Dan brushed

her roughly aside, leaped to his feet, and ran into the hallway. Redd could only have gone out the back way and down the stairs. Ragan legged it down the corridor the short distance to the exit and out onto the narrow landing. The man working on the buggy was staring in the direction of the hitch rack. It could only be the outlaw, racing down the steps and onto his horse, that had attracted his attention.

Ragan darted back into the hallway and ran its length to the first of the rooms. Entering, he rushed across to the window and looked down. The outlaw was just swinging up into the saddle. Dan leveled his gun at the sharp-faced man.

"Redd—don't try it!"

The outlaw rocked sideways on his horse, pistol suddenly in his hand. He glanced up, his features taut and distorted. "The hell with you!" he shouted, triggering his weapon.

The bullet shattered the glass of the window above Ragan and thudded into the wall beyond him.

"Give it up, Redd—you'll never make it!" Dan called again.

But the outlaw, already wheeling away from the shying horses at the rack, shook his head and sent another bullet at Ragan.

Grim, Dan lurched to one side and steadied his pistol. As Arlie Redd jammed spurs into the flanks of the bay and twisted about for another, final shot, Ragan squeezed off the trigger of his forty-five. The outlaw stiffened as the slug tore into him. His horse, slowing when the hand on the reins faltered, came to a stop. A moment later Arlie Redd slid from the saddle and fell heavily to the ground.

21

Dashing away the sweat misting his eyes, Ragan spun, hurried across the room to the doorway, entered the corridor, and ran to the stairs. Redd was down, and he had no fear of the outlaw escaping now, but he did have hopes of finding out from the man before he died—if he wasn't already dead —where his two remaining partners were. He had assumed that all four had been heading for Kansas, with Dodge City their specific destination, but Kitchens and Redd had been at the way station. It could be the others were going to some different point also.

The woman in the yellow dress was halfway down the steps as he started to descend, and as he rushed past her taking several steps at a time, she muttered something and gave him a hating look.

Ragan paid no attention, and reaching floor level, he began to shoulder his way through the crowd now shifting toward the door. He reached the landing and hastily turned the corner of the saloon and ran to where Arlie Redd lay.

Ignoring the half-a-dozen persons gathered around the fallen outlaw, Ragan crouched beside him. Unbuttoning Redd's shirt, he relieved him of the bulging money belt, new as Dave Kitchens', and then removed the roll of currency that he was carrying in a shirt pocket.

Ragan, the cash safely in his possession, bent low over the outlaw and felt for a pulse. Redd was still alive but was dying fast. Putting his mouth close to the man's ear, Dan shook him roughly.

"Arlie—where's Ed Peabody? Where was he going?"

The outlaw's eyes fluttered, opened. A frown corrugated his forehead. "Dave? He . . . he . . . dead?"

Ragan nodded. Redd's eyes closed, then opened again as Dan shook him once more.

"You're dying too. You can do those folks back in Texas a big favor—same as you can do something good for yourself—if you'll talk up. Tell me where I can find Ed and Rufe, so's I can get the rest of the money."

Redd frowned. His mouth worked convulsively and faint words came from his dry lips. Ragan bent lower to catch the weak reply.

"Dodge . . . We was all . . . headed . . . for Dodge. Me and Dave . . . laid over . . . here. Was a woman . . . I knowed . . . back in—"

The outlaw's voice dropped even lower, and he finally became silent. Ragan looked more closely at the man, again feeling for a pulse. This time there was none—the outlaw was dead.

Rising, Dan stood for a moment looking out over the heat shimmering flats west of the town. Relief was running through him; he had learned where the other outlaws could be found. Turning, he started for the saloon, suddenly bone-tired and sagging from lack of sleep. Reaching the door, he entered and moved up to the bar, the crowd of eighteen or twenty persons at his heels.

"Can use a drink," he said to the barkeep.

The man behind the counter poured a shot glass full of whiskey, placed it before Ragan, and then shoved the belt taken off Kitchens alongside it.

"Was altogether seven thousand four hundred and twenty dollars there," he said, glancing at the figures he had scribbled onto a scrap of paper. "It's all in the belt."

Ragan nodded and tossed off the drink. Tension had ebbed from him now, but the grimness still remained. Taking up the belt he hung it across his shoulder with that of Arlie Redd's.

"Obliged to you. There a lawman around here?"

"Nope," the bartender said. "Ain't nobody'll take the job."

Dan considered that for a long breath and then shrugged. "Appreciate it if you'll see that there's a burying. Probably enough money in their pockets to pay for it. If not, you can sell their horses and gear."

"Why the hell don't you take them, too?" a man standing near the doorway asked. "You done stripped them of their belts. Might as well grab everything else they own."

"Just might do that," Ragan drawled, turning about and hooking his elbows on the edge of the bar. He was in no mood to listen to some bleeding heart bleating over the deaths of a couple of killers. "But I don't figure it's worth the trouble."

196

"Just cash money—that's all you want—"

"What I want is seventy-five hundred dollars from each one of them. That's how much of the stolen money they had. I doubt if there's that much in Redd's belt—there wasn't in Kitchens'—and that's what I expected. They've had time to do some spending—but I'm calling it even."

Ragan, having made his explanation, came back around and motioned for another drink. The crowd began to break up, some returning to the tables, others moving on through the doorway to the outside and heading for the other saloons and the way-station depot from which they had come when the excitement began.

But there were two men who continued to hang around, listening to what was being said and watching Dan Ragan with narrow interest. It came to him as he finished off his second drink that he now had on his person a lot of money—somewhere in the neighborhood of fifteen thousand dollars—and that was bound to be an attraction to some. If he expected to get the money back to those people in Texas—and stay alive—he'd need to take precautions. The cash should be changed into a draft—but the nearest bank was in Dodge City. That meant he'd have to

197

manage until he got there—and judging from the attention he was being accorded by the two hardcases, he'd best start being careful now.

Thrusting the belts inside his shirt, Dan nodded to the bartender. "Aim to get a bite to eat and then grab myself some shut-eye. After that I'll be lining out for Colorado —Trinidad," he said in a voice neither too loud nor too low. "It much of a ride?"

"Day if a man's in a hurry. Day and a half if he takes it easy," the barkeep replied, leaning forward slightly. "Them two jaspers over there by the wall—they're real tough *hombres,*" he continued in a whisper. "Tall one's Nate Walcott. Other'n's Pete Orlich. Seen them watching you like they was getting ideas. I'd sure keep a sharp eye on them, was I you."

Ragan expressed his appreciation of the warning with a nod, and taking a coin from a side pocket, dropped it on the counter to pay for his drinks.

"When'll you be riding out?" the barkeep asked.

"First light, probably," Ragan answered, and moving away from the bar, returned to his horse. Mounting, he rode the short distance to the stable at the rear of the stage depot.

A hostler appeared almost at once, an elderly man with a florid, closely shaved face. Taking the sorrel's bridle in his hand, he waited for Ragan to leave the saddle.

"You staying all night?" he asked.

Dan nodded, and gave his instructions for the care of the gelding as he removed his saddlebags. He started to turn away, then hesitated, his eyes on a shotgun standing in the corner of the stableman's quarters.

"That scattergun in good working order?"

The hostler turned to look at the weapon, then said, "Sure is. Why?"

The barrels of the shotgun had been sawed off and it appeared to be a twelve-gauge. It would suit his purpose ideally, Dan thought.

"I'll give you a double eagle for it and a dozen shells. Got an extra six-gun I'll throw in for good measure."

The stableman bobbed. "You got a deal, mister! Way business's been I'd sell my old woman for twenty dollars, almost."

The man disappeared into his office, returning shortly with the weapon and a handful of shells, all buckshot load. Ragan broke the gun, peered into its twin barrels, and tested the triggers. It was old but in good condition. Paying the hostler, he slipped shells into the chambers of both barrels, and hanging the weapon in the crook of his left arm, walked the short distance to the depot. Entering by the rear door, he went immediately to the section set aside as a restaurant, and selecting a corner table, ordered a big meal.

Sleep was pressing him hard, reminding him that he'd closed his eyes only fitfully during the last few days and nights and that he could not go much longer without it. To try and do so would be foolish. With luck he had sidetracked any of those in the saloon who had plans to ambush him when he rode out by sending them off in the wrong direction, but he still would need to be wide awake and on constant alert once he got on the trail.

Hunger satisfied, he rose and crossed to the counter at the front of the room and paid his check. "I'm needing a room for the night," he said when that matter had been taken care of. "You the man I see about it?"

The clerk, young, small-eyed, dark hair parted in the center, nodded, his gaze fixed on the sawed-off shotgun Ragan was carrying.

"Yes, sir. . . . You the fellow that done them killings over at the Cactus Rose?"

Ragan brushed off the question. "What about a room?" he pressed coldly.

"Yes, sir," the clerk said again. He pushed a dog-eared ledger and stub of a pencil across the counter to Dan. "You'd be him, all right. . . . How long you staying?"

"Till morning," Ragan replied, registering. "How much?"

"Be a dollar," the clerk said. Unhooking a key from a board affixed to the wall behind him, he handed it to Dan. "You'll be wanting a door with a good lock. That'll be number five."

Ragan nodded, laid a silver dollar on the counter, and headed down the hallway off the small lobby.

"Third door to your left," the clerk called helpfully.

Dan again nodded. A bed was going to feel mighty good—but he had no intentions of staying in it for the entire night. He expected to be up and on the trail long before first light.

22

Ragan rode into Dodge City around mid-morning several days later. His deception had apparently worked, as he had seen no sign of Walcott or Pete Orlich—or any other riders who had plans to bushwhack and rob him. With luck he had shaken all outlaws with such ideas for good—and that was something Dan would like to believe; there had already been too much killing.

It was unlikely, however, that there would be no more shooting. Peabody and Cobb would not surrender their shares of the ranchers' money without a fight—and Dan was determined to recover it. But it would be up to them. Just as it had been with Dave Kitchens and Arlie Redd, he'd offer them the opportunity to hand over the money. If they refused and chose to shoot it out, he would have no choice but to use his gun and trust that he would come out winner.

Two upright posts supporting a sign met him as he turned into the end of the main street: THE CARRYING OF FIREARMS STRICTLY PROHIBITED, it warned in bold, black letters. Ragan drew his weapon from its holster and thrust it under his belt, thus removing it from sight.

Earlier he had taken the two money belts and placed them in the bottom of his saddlebags, covering them well with the contents already in the leather pouches. As soon as he found Peabody and Cobb, assuming they were still in Dodge, and recovered the money they had, assuming —again—that he could do so and live, he'd look up a bank and get the cash converted to a draft. He'd rest a lot easier once that was done.

Off to the south of town where lay the railroad and the stock-loading pens, Ragan could hear the bawling of cattle and reckoned a trail drive had come to an end and the beef was being loaded. He'd been to Dodge only once before, and glancing about now as he rode down the center of the street, he was surprised at all the change marking the town's growth.

There looked to be more saloons than ever, but too, there were signs now of civilization—a newspaper, more general stores, gun and saddle shops, restaurants, offices, hotels, and such. The street was fairly busy, with buggies, wagons, and riders on horseback continually on the move while pedestrians trod the sidewalks. Finding Ed Peabody and Rufe Cobb was not going to be easy, he realized; he had visualized Dodge City as he remembered it—a settlement of a few hundred, not of several thousand.

Abruptly a man in a blue suit and wearing a star that said CITY POLICE stepped off the board walk, and raising a hand, confronted him. Ragan drew the sorrel to a stop.

"Where you headed?" the lawman asked. Clean-shaven except for a thick, black mustache, he had small, cold blue eyes.

"Just got here," Dan replied. "It against the law to ride down the street?"

"It's against the law to be carrying a gun," the policeman said crisply. "Can see your holster's empty—but I can see the bulge in your shirt, too, where you're packing it. Now, if you're aiming to stay in Dodge, you check that gun at the jail, or leave it in your room."

Ragan made no reply. Several persons on

the nearby sidewalk had paused, listening with interest. A second lawman appeared, this one a solid-looking individual in a gray suit and wearing a star that designated him as the city marshal.

"Some trouble here, Jim?" he asked, moving up beside the policeman.

"No, nothing much," the lawman replied. "Just telling this stranger we don't allow any gun packing inside the town limits. He's got his stuck inside his shirt."

The marshal's features hardened. "You got a reason for doing that, mister?"

Ragan said, "Not specially. Just got here and—"

"Well, either you put that iron in your saddlebags or leave it in your room, once you get one. Otherwise, take it down to the jail and check it with one of my deputies. Goes for that shotgun hanging from your saddlehorn, too. Mind telling me your name?"

"Dan Ragan. Came here looking for two men. Personal business. Names are Peabody and Cobb. Peabody's a big fellow. Was riding a gray gelding last time I saw him. Cobb—"

"Try the other side of the Dead Line," the policeman suggested, pointing toward the railroad tracks. "Seems I recollect seeing a man answering that description over there yesterday."

"Obliged," Ragan said, and rode on.

The area south of the gleaming rails was a huddled collection of saloons and bawdy-houses with a few restaurants and small businesses thrown in for the benefit and convenience of those who decided they needed something besides liquor, women, and gambling. It existed solely for the use of trail hands and others seeking unrestricted amusement, and at the moment, although it was not yet noon—much less evening— activity was in full swing.

Halting in front of the first saloon, Dan tied the sorrel to the rack and stepped up onto the landing that fronted the structure. Peabody's gray horse was not anywhere along the street, but the man could have walked over from the main part of Dodge, or he might have stabled the animal in one of the barns behind the numerous saloons.

Dan realized he could do nothing but start his search and hope that somewhere along the way he'd encounter the two outlaws. Failing to find them on this side of the Dead Line, he'd have no choice but to return to Dodge City proper and make the rounds there.

Ragan had not considered what he would do then if he was unable to turn up either of the men in Dodge. They had been heading for it—which was customary for men looking for excitement—and he had given no thought to the possibility of their not being there.

Dan had always figured himself for a man who usually had good luck, and it held true that hot summer morning. As he entered the crowded, noisy, smoke-filled room and bulled his way to a place at the bar, a hard smile crossed his lips. Rufe Cobb was sitting with a woman at one of the tables in the back of the room.

Tension drawing him tight, Ragan ordered a drink from the bartender. While he waited, he reached into his shirt, procured his pistol, and dropped it into its holster. Evidently the no-gun law did not apply to this side of the Dead Line, as every man present in the saloon was armed.

Taking up his drink, Dan turned and slowly probed the room for a glimpse of Peabody. It was to no avail. The big outlaw was not there—but Rufe Cobb was and that filled Dan Ragan with satisfaction. Peabody would not be far away.

Finishing off his whiskey, Ragan moved

out into the crowd of milling patrons, and circling close to the wall, came in behind Cobb. The woman with the outlaw, dark-haired, dark-eyed, with a high, full bosom, glanced up questioningly. Dan shook his head and sat down on a chair at the next table. Drawing his weapon, he leaned forward and jammed the muzzle of the forty-five into Cobb's back. Rufe stiffened, slowly raising his arms.

"Keep your hands down—flat on the table," Dan ordered in a low voice. "And don't make any sudden moves. I could pull this trigger and nobody'd hear it in all this racket."

Cobb complied quickly. "Who the hell are you?" he demanded hoarsely. "What do you want?"

"Seventy-five hundred dollars—your share of the money you and your *compadres* took away from the Hurley gang. That answer your question?"

Cobb had twisted slowly about. His eyes met Ragan's hard, unrelenting features. His mouth sagged. "You—" he mumbled.

"Yeh, me," Dan said. "Only need to collect from you and Peabody, then I can take all the money back to the folks it belongs to. Now, look straight ahead and don't move your hands. I'm going to take your money belt, then I'll see what's in your pockets. Keep remembering how easy it'll be for my gun to go off."

Cobb swore deeply.

"You sure'n hell ain't going to get away with this—"

"Aim to try," Dan replied coolly, "and if I don't, you'll come out with the worst of it. . . . Don't," he added warningly to the dark-eyed woman as she started to rise. "Just stay right where you are."

As she settled back, Ragan slipped a hand inside the outlaw's shirt and, releasing the buckle, drew the money belt free. Thrusting it inside his own garment, he glanced around. Activity in the saloon had not slackened and all was as it had been. No one had taken even the smallest note of what was transpiring at the corner table.

Ragan edged forward a bit farther, reaching into the outlaw's pocket. His fingers touched a roll of bills, one much smaller than those taken off Redd and Kitchens.

"This all there is?"

Rufe nodded and swore again. The outlaw was sweating heavily and when he looked around there was a wildness in his eyes.

"Yeh, damn you to hell, you bastard —that's all!"

"He done some gambling—lost," the woman said, helpfully. "Told him not—"

"Shut up!" Cobb snarled. "Keep your stinking lip to yourself!"

Dan tucked the currency into his shirt pocket. "Where's Peabody?" he asked, still at low voice. "Telling me will save me some time. Don't tell me and I'll find him anyway."

The outlaw twisted half about. "I ain't telling you nothing! You can go plumb to hell for—" Cobb's words broke off in midsentence. He straightened in his chair, glance reaching beyond Ragan to the saloon's entrance.

"Ed—it's that holy-joe cowhand!" he shouted. "Get the hell out of here!"

Peabody! Dan pivoted on his chair. The big outlaw stood framed in the doorway of the saloon, halted by his partner's warning. Instantly Peabody whirled. Ragan lunged to his feet but Cobb caught him by the arm, jerking him back.

Off balance, Dan swore angrily and swinging the forty-five hard, clubbed Rufe viciously on the side of the head. The outlaw groaned and released his grip. Immediately

210

recovering himself, Ragan rushed off through the crowded room in pursuit of Peabody.

23

Ragan gained the saloon's landing, pulled up short, and glanced hurriedly around for Peabody. A gray horse had just crossed the tracks, veering into one of Dodge's side streets.

Dan delayed no longer. Peabody was there. All that remained was to nail him before he could disappear. Yanking the sorrel's reins free, Dan swung onto the saddle, and raking the surprised gelding with his spurs, sent the big horse racing off in the wake of the outlaw.

Peabody had not stood and fought as Ragan had expected him to do. He knew the outlaw was not a man to back off, and his actions puzzled Dan. The answer came to him suddenly; Ed Peabody was unarmed. Apparently striving to stay on good terms with the law in Dodge, he—and probably Rufe Cobb—were not carrying guns.

The sorrel hurdled the rails in a long, low jump, and at Ragan's direction swerved left into a ragged lane that passed as a street. Dan swore. The outlaw was not in sight. Drawing the sorrel down to a fast walk, he continued, eyes whipping from side to side as he sought to locate Peabody.

A bit of hanging dust at the far end of a vacant lot drew his attention. There was a chance it could have been made by the outlaw—and there was nothing else to go on. Cutting the sorrel sharp right, Dan angled across the square of open, weedy ground toward the yellowish pall.

He came out in an alley lying behind a row of stores—and there was Peabody. He saw the outlaw several hundred yards on up the way, turning into a passageway between two of the buildings. Such would bring him out onto the street that fronted the business houses.

Ignoring the alley, Ragan spurred directly to the street. By doing so he would be in a position to see Peabody when he emerged from the passage.

The sorrel reached the street at a hard, driving run. Dan swung him into it and threw his glance along the row of buildings. At that moment he saw the outlaw spurt into the open, veer left, and duck into the wide, open doorway of a livery barn.

Ragan grinned tightly. Peabody evidently intended to hide out in the stable. With his horse near, he could lie low until such time as he felt it was safe to move, and then joined by Cobb, ride on. But Peabody was due for a hell of a big surprise, Ragan vowed as he rode along the fairly busy street toward the livery stable. He'd never leave—

"Hold it, Ragan!"

Dan brought the gelding to a quick stop. Anger and frustration swept him when he saw the lawman—the stocky one with the city-marshal badge—come out of a store, and hand resting on the pistol riding his hip, slowly approach.

"You was told about wearing that forty-five," the marshal said. "And you still got that scattergun hanging from your saddle. Seems you figure you're somebody special."

Ragan cursed himself silently. He'd forgotten all about the shotgun, and after he'd buffaloed Rufe Cobb with his pistol and took off after Ed Peabody, he'd shoved the weapon back into its holster—again forgetting about the no-weapons rule inside

214

the town's limits.

"Real sorry about that, Marshal," he said. "Was over across the tracks and slipped my mind—"

"That ain't likely," the lawman cut in coldly. "Expect the truth is you're looking to gun somebody down, and it's my job to stop you. Climb down off that horse. We're taking a walk over to the jail."

Ragan did not stir. "Slipped my mind, just like I said, Marshal. And right now I've got important business to—"

"Nothing's more important to me than keeping the peace here in Dodge," the lawman snapped. "Now, you coming along peaceable or am I calling for a couple of my deputies and dragging you in?"

Dan looked closely at the marshal. The lawman was now holding a pistol in his hand, and there was a hard set to the man's jaw. It was clear that arguing with him would gain nothing. Shrugging, hand well away from his own weapon, Ragan came off the sorrel. Immediately the marshal relieved him of his pistol.

"Now, march," the lawman commanded. "Lead your horse. You can stable him in the barn behind the jail till I get this thing sorted out."

"Throwing me in's going to let an outlaw —a killer—get away," Ragan said, moving off down the street with the marshal at his shoulder. "Trailed him here from New Mexico and had just spotted him when you—"

"What's his name?"

"Ed Peabody. He and three other—"

"I don't recollect no warrants on an Ed Peabody, or a wanted dodger either."

"Maybe so, but he's plenty well known over in Texas and New Mexico. He's got over seven thousand dollars on him right now—his share of thirty thousand stolen from another bunch of outlaws who killed and robbed a trail boss and—"

"Sounds a mite mixed up," the lawman said. "Turn right at that saddle shop. Jail's on just a ways."

Ragan sighed. He was getting nowhere with the marshal, and once locked in a cell he'd make even less headway. Ed Peabody would escape, and this time, aware that he was being sought, would take pains to drop out of sight.

Dan slowed. Two riders had entered the street at its upper end. Eyes narrowing, he studied the pair. It was Orlich and Walcott, the two *hombres* from the way station.

Discovering they had been tricked into believing he had ridden north from the way station, they had doubled back and taken the only logical alternate course—east, and they had arrived at the worst possible time. Or had they?

Ragan's mind moved quickly. Perhaps he could turn the presence of the two hardcases to his advantage. He glanced about. The street—actually more an alley—alongside the saddle shop into which they were turning was narrow and cluttered with boxes and crates and empty whiskey barrels from a nearby saloon.

A horse stood hitched to a post close to the rear of the saddlery, and the realization came to Ragan that if he was to avoid being locked up in a Dodge City jail and losing Ed Peabody and the rest of the stolen money, he must act now.

"Marshal," he said, coming to a stop and pointing at Walcott and Orlich who, having spotted him, had also halted, "there's a couple of jaspers that I know for damn sure you've got dodgers on."

The lawman frowned, brushed at the sweat on his face. "This another one of your long-winded yarns about—"

"No—it's the truth."

217

"Maybe. Who are—"

The marshal never got the question completely voiced. Hating to do it, but desperate, Ragan lunged against the marshal, knocking him hard into a jumble of boxes and crates. As the lawman went down, Dan made a grab for the pistol he was holding —missed. There was no time for a second try—and he still had the old double barrel slung from his saddle. Pivoting fast, he vaulted onto the sorrel and sent him thundering down the littered side street.

He heard the marshal yell out as he reached the end of the alleyway, and heard the sharp crack of a gunshot as he cut left into another alleylike lane. He didn't know where the bullet had gone, but luck had been with him and he had gotten clear in time.

But good fortune otherwise was not favoring him. He would now have all of Dodge City's lawmen looking for him, as well as Pete Orlich and Nate Walcott. And adding to those, he could plan on Rufe Cobb, sided by Ed Peabody, to try and recover the money taken from him.

The solution was to move fast and get the hell out of Dodge. If he could keep the town law force off his back, he could handle the others—and the first move toward that end

218

was to close in on Peabody, hiding in the livery stable on the next street.

With the sound of shouting back near the saddle shop in his ears, Ragan made a wide circle around several close-by buildings, thus avoiding not only the curious persons hurrying to see what the marshal was yelling about, but the two hardcases—Walcott and Orlich—as well.

He'd have a tough time shaking them now, Dan knew, but he'd manage. Right now it was Ed Peabody that he must deal with—and that moment of confrontation was at hand. The rear of the livery stable was directly ahead.

24

Ragan slowed the sorrel, walked him in close to the rear of the broad, slanted-roof building, and drew to a halt a few steps from the partly open door. Coming quietly off the saddle, he unhooked the shotgun from the horn, taking a minute to remove the rawhide thong with which he'd suspended the weapon, and then broke it softly to check its loads. Both barrels of the twelve-gauge were ready. Muffling the click as he snapped the weapon shut and holding it crosswise in front of him, he moved up to the doorway. Hesitating for a moment, he took a deep breath and quickly stepped inside.

The cool darkness of the stable's interior was hushed and filled with the odors of fresh hay, oiled leather, and horse droppings. Pulled back in the deep shadows along the wall, Ragan listened while his eyes searched the runway directly before him.

The front entrance to the barn was open and the square of light being admitted set the area between the stalls on each side into sharp focus. There was no one visible in the runway, but somewhere along its length Dan could hear movement. Straining, he tried to determine the nature of the sound; could it be a man—Peabody perhaps—readying his mount to ride out? Ragan decided that such was unlikely, that it was probably no more than a restless horse stirring about in his stall.

The outlaw could have come and gone, Dan realized as he stood motionless in the darkness. He had simply assumed the man was ducking into the livery stable to hide. Instead, he could very well have ridden on through—and escaped.

To where? Which way would Peabody be most inclined to ride if he chose to leave Dodge? And would he go without his partner, Rufe Cobb? The answer to the latter question came easily. There was small loyalty between outlaws and where a large amount of money was at stake there would be none at all. Ed Peabody would do what he figured was best for Ed Peabody, and to hell with

221

Rufe Cobb or anyone else who—

"I ain't waiting no longer—"

The voice that broke the silence in the stable came suddenly from near the front of the building. It brought Ragan to quick attention. Moments later a heavily built figure stepped out into the runway from what was likely the proprietor's office. It was Peabody.

"Can tell him I'm heading up Wichita way."

The outlaw was apparently speaking of Cobb whom he had expected to join him at the stable. Peabody was now wearing his gun, and as he stood silhouetted against the opening at the end of the runway he made some sort of adjustment with the belt's buckle. Evidently, in deference to the law, he had left his weapon at the stable and was now reclaiming it.

"Get my horse—"

"Sure."

The hostler's reply was barely audible as he came out of the office and turned into the runway.

"Got him ready, just like you was wanting."

Ragan waited until the man was well clear of the big outlaw and then moving forward out of the shadows, took up a position at the edge of the lane. The hostler pulled up short when he saw Dan, and his eyes widened as he looked into the twin muzzles of the sawed-off shotgun.

Ragan, warning the man to keep quiet, motioned him into the nearest stall. The hostler obeyed quickly. At that instant Peabody came about.

"You!" he yelled in anger and surprise as he saw Ragan; dipping slightly to one side, he went for the pistol on his hip.

Dan swung the double-barrel around, pressing off the forward trigger. The charge of buckshot lifted Peabody off his feet, slamming him back against the wall while the blast of the weapon, coupled with that of the outlaw's gun, rocked the stable and filled the runway with a swirling cloud of powder smoke.

Ragan, crouched against the dividing timber of two stalls, felt a warm wetness on his leg. He had not been aware that Peabody's bullet had hit him—and it barely had. A quarter inch more to the left and it would have bypassed him entirely. As it was, it had cut a furrow along the outside of his leg midway between knee and hip.

"Is—is he dead?"

Dan shrugged as the hostler's question reached him, and moving away from the upright, he crossed to where Peabody lay. A warning was running through him; he would need to act fast. The reports of the shotgun and the pistol would carry, and with Dodge City's lawmen all out searching for him, one or more were bound to have heard and hasten to investigate.

Kneeling beside Peabody, ignoring the stinging sensation in his leg, Ragan removed the money belt from the outlaw's waist, dug a small roll of bills from his side pocket, and drew himself upright.

"This money was stole from a man—a trail boss—down in Texas," he said to the gaping hostler. "I'm taking it back to the folks it belongs to."

The stableman nodded woodenly. Ragan, reaching down, retrieved the outlaw's weapon, thumbed out the spent cartridge, and glanced at it. A forty-five—the same caliber as his gun—taken from him a few minutes earlier by the marshal.

"I'm taking the gun—he won't be needing it where he's going," Dan said, sliding the weapon into his holster. "Something else— when the law asks you about this be damn sure you tell it straight. It was a fair fight."

"Yes, sir, it sure was," the stableman said in a tight voice.

Instantly Ragan wheeled. A change in the man's eyes and expression had sent a warning through him. As he turned, he rocked to one side. The figure hurtling at him from the doorway of the livery stable office went plunging by to crash shoulder first into an unyielding post.

Rufe Cobb! Ragan, shotgun leveled, stepped quickly to the groaning outlaw laying in the dung and straw on the stable floor. He recoiled as he looked up at Ragan.

"Don't shoot! I'm hurt bad—shoulder—busted!"

It was probably the truth, Dan thought. The outlaw had charged full force into the thick upright at the end of a stall.

"All right," Ragan snapped, feeling more and more the need to leave, to get away from the barn before some lawman could put in an appearance. "I'll let it end here, forget who and what you are, Rufe—but if we ever meet again I'll finish what I started here. Savvy?"

Cobb nodded weakly. Dan turned, the pain in his leg now a steady throbbing, and walking hurriedly down the runway, reached the back door. He did not pause, having no fear of either man since both were unarmed, and stepping outside, crossed to the waiting sorrel. As he swung stiffly onto the saddle, the sound of voices coming from inside the stable reached him.

"Out the back!" he heard Rufe Cobb yell. "He went out the back way."

Ragan swore. It was as he'd feared. The gunshots had been heard and the law had come to see what it was all about. Pivoting the sorrel, he sent the big horse rushing off down the alley that lay behind the stable.

He had recovered all of the money—at least as much as it was possible to get back—and he was feeling good about that. But there was still the matter of leaving Dodge and returning to Texas with it. He'd have no opportunity now to convert the cash into a draft; he'd simply have to carry it as it was.

The immediate problem, however, was slipping by the lawmen who watched over the town and avoiding Nate Walcott and his partner, Pete Orlich. They had spotted him at the time he'd caught sight of them and knew that he was in Dodge.

The alley ended in an open field a short distance from the center of the town. There was little cover, and at once Dan cut back toward a house on his left. No one had set out in pursuit of him after he'd ridden away from the stable, and he reckoned whoever it was that had shown up to investigate the gunshots had been delayed in getting a horse or summoning other lawmen.

That was to his favor. It gave him that much more time to get out of Dodge and lose himself in the hilly country to the south and west. Halting near the house, Dan glanced about to get his directions straight. The river—the Arkansas—should be on straight ahead, to the south. Once he crossed it he could feel that he was on his way.

Doubtless the marshal, whoever he might be, was plenty riled at him for escaping as he had, but it would be more a matter of injured pride than anything else, since there had been no crime involved; and the lawman, failing to find his temporary prisoner inside the town's limits was not likely to mount a posse for a search beyond.

Ragan moved on, now keeping close to the row of houses that stood between him and the main part of Dodge. His leg was paining him considerably, and he knew that something would have to be done soon. When he reached the Arkansas, he'd pull up and tend to it as best he could by cleaning it with water, disinfecting it by pouring a bit of whiskey from his bottle into it, and then applying a bandage. That should hold it until he reached a town where there was a doctor. He was still running in luck, he thought; the wound could have been serious.

Glancing ahead, Dan could see the silver shine of the river through the trees that grew along its banks. Here and there wagons, their arching canvas tops stark white in the bleaching sunlight, had been halted while their passengers sought brief rest from their tiring westward journey.

Staying clear of the camps, Dan rode up to the river and pulled into a pocket amid the brush and trees. The Arkansas was low, and he could hear children shouting and laughing as they played in the shallows. Letting the sorrel satisfy his thirst, Ragan set to work doctoring his wounded leg. He'd been able to avoid Dodge City's lawmen so far, and for that he was grateful, but the knowledge that Orlich and Walcott were still unaccounted for filled him with an uneasiness and kept him on the alert.

Finished with dressing his wound, Dan turned to the problem of effectively hiding the money he was carrying. After some thought he took the sack of grain he'd brought along for the gelding and, pouring most of the remainder out, placed the packs of currency and the gold coins that made up the near thirty thousand dollars in the sack and then added the grain he had removed. By shifting the cash about he succeeded in covering it all with oats and ended up with what appeared to be a sack of horse feed hanging from the horn of his saddle.

He reckoned he was ready to head south for Texas when that was done and, favoring his stiff but not too uncomfortable leg, went up onto the sorrel's back and rode him back to higher ground.

Ragan drew to a stop, a frown pulling at his whisker-stubbled face. Two riders were coming toward him: Nate Walcott and Pete Orlich. They were moving along the river bank, eying the camps. Undoubtedly they were searching for him. Either they intended to make a complete circle of the town, hoping to catch sight of him as he rode out, or else reasoned that Ragan, having come up from Texas and New Mexico, would be heading back in the same direction.

Whatever, here they were, and Dan Ragan, seeing in them the last barrier to returning the money to the people he had unknowingly deprived of it, considered the two outlaws with cold, narrow eyes.

The advantage was his. They were still unaware of his presence, while he was in a position to blow them off their saddles if he so wished and thus make certain they would never again pose a problem to him—or anyone else for that matter. He had but to sit quietly in the deep brush until they had drawn abreast, then shout his challenge, and, as they went for their weapons, use the shotgun.

And thereby add two more to the number of deaths the money had caused.

Ragan considered that soberly as he studied the outlaws. After a bit he shrugged. There'd been enough killing—and these could be avoided. Backing the sorrel deeper into the brush, he sat motionless as the outlaws passed by, all the while hoping that nothing would occur to attract their attention and force him to use the old double-barrel again.

And luck, as if weary, too, of the killing, was with him once again. Orlich and Walcott, their voices barely audible as they moved slowly by the certain death that awaited them should they turn and glance in Ragan's direction, did not look around but continued on their way.

Remaining where he was until the two hardcases were out of sight, Dan doubled back to the higher ground, and crossing the Arkansas at the ford, pointed the sorrel south for Texas.

25

Sacksville appeared to be a mighty fine town, Dan Ragan thought as he topped out a wooded hill and looked down on the settlement sprawled in a grassy valley. It was fairly large, too, as towns went, having a population of maybe five or six thousand persons plus those living on the ranches and homesteads he'd noticed along the way as he drew nearer.

The long ride from Dodge had been uneventful, except for a bit of trouble in that panhandle strip off the Indian Territory folks called No Man's Land, so named because of the lawless element that holed up there. Two Mexican *vaqueros,* probably left over from a cattle drive and now hiding from the law for some reason, apparently had need of a horse. They attempted to steal his

232

sorrel, but Ragan, anticipating their intentions, had driven them off. The pair, one with a charge of buckshot in his hind quarters, did not trouble him again.

But it was about over now: the grief, the tension, the sheer hard labor involved at times, and the killing, were at an end. He had but to ride in, find the sheriff's office and hand him the feed sack with the money. Then he could wipe it all from his mind and go about the business of finding himself a job.

He could forget Wyoming. He was a good ten or twelve days late now and it would take another ten days or so to ride back. Such would be for nothing. J. J. Hamilton had made it clear that he'd hold the foreman job open only until the day specified as a deadline arrived. After that he would be forced to hire someone else.

And Cameo Wakefield—her sisters—and the Circle W ranch. That chance was down the well, too. With the deaths of both their father and uncle, who had together operated the spread, they had needed help at once—a fact that Cameo had made clear to him.

He'd missed his opportunity for being somebody, for becoming the boss of a big ranch where Hamilton was concerned, and as for the Wakefields, where he might one day have become part owner of the spread, not as large an outfit as the Double J, true, but with fine prospects—he'd lost out there also.

But he reckoned he'd live through it. He had done what he felt he must, and while it had cost him his future, Dan had no regrets. At least he could sleep nights without his conscience nagging him.

Raking the gelding lightly with his spurs, he headed down slope for the town. Reaching the first of the houses, scattered about on all four sides of the business district, he entered the main street—clean, wide, and well shaded by huge pecan, chinaberry, and sycamore trees.

Persons along the way turned to eye him curiously as he passed, some smiling, others merely giving him their glance. He paid them little mind, his thoughts being centered on locating the office of Sheriff Sam Avery and discharging the last of his self-imposed duties.

He found the combination jail and lawman's office just short of the town's center and pulled up to the rack fronting it. Swinging down from the saddle, he unhooked the feed sack from the horn, and hanging it over a shoulder, entered the narrow building, heavy with heat at mid-afternoon.

Avery was sitting behind a desk, rummaging through a sheaf of papers. He glanced up, smiled quickly, and came to his feet.

"By God, Ragan—it's you!"

Dan nodded, dropping the feed sack on the desk. "Sure is. Money's all there 'cepting some they'd already spent by the time I'd caught up with them."

Arm extended, smile growing wider, Avery came out from back of his desk and shook Ragan's hand vigorously.

"Told folks around here what you was doing. Most of them wouldn't believe it —said we'd never see or hear from you again. This here's going to do me a lot of good—watching them eat crow. . . . Hold on a minute—"

Avery stepped to the door, halted a passerby. "Go get Tom Gilpin. Tell him I said to come over here fast. This fellow's brought back the money them outlaws took off Jim Drayson."

The man hurried away, yelling something to another bystander as he went. The sheriff came back to Dan.

"Gilpin runs the bank here. Can turn the

money over to him to pay off those folks. . . . My friend, you're going to be a mighty big man hereabouts—a real hero! Set down and let's do some jawing about what happened after I left you that night."

Ragan settled onto the chair the lawman indicated and, bolstered by a drink of whiskey from the quart bottle Avery took from a drawer in his desk, brushed lightly over the incidents that had ended with him recovering the last of the money in Dodge City. When he had finished, Sam Avery sighed deeply, almost enviously.

"You sure had yourself a time, and it appears you come out with a whole hide and in good shape. But I'm wondering about something; I recollect you was heading out to take on a fine job. What about that?"

"Was two jobs—and I was trying to make up my mind which one I wanted. Both just sort of got lost in the shuffle."

"Too bad," Avery murmured. "You got any prospects?"

"Might could go back to Axhead—ranch where I'd been working—but I got my doubts. They had too much hired help then and I figure the boss was glad to see me quit."

"Times are plenty tough, all right," Avery

agreed. "Lot of men looking for work. See them go through here every day—but maybe I got a idea."

"Idea?"

"Yeh. I've got the whole county to look after and it ain't always easy for folks around here 'cause I'm gone a lot. The bigwigs told me to hire myself a deputy any time I wanted." Avery paused, looked closely at Dan. "You interested?"

Ragan stared back at the lawman. "Me be a deputy sheriff?"

"Yep. Pay's good—sixty a month along with room and board. And a fellow can pick hisself up a reward every now and then."

Ragan frowned, shook his head. "Hell, I don't know anything about being a lawman. I—"

"You can handle a gun," Avery said, "and you got something bettcr'n experience—you got a natural feeling for what's right and what's wrong and that's what makes a top grade lawman. What do you say?"

Dan raised his eyes and looked out into the street. A crowd was approaching the jail led by the man Avery had dispatched for the banker, and another man in a business suit —the banker Gilpin, he supposed. Everyone

237

appeared excited and others were joining the procession as it advanced.

"Seems half the town's coming to shake your hand," Avery observed. "Sure would pleasure me to tell them when they get here that you're hiring on as my deputy—and that you'll be in charge of things around here when I'm gone."

Dan Ragan continued to gaze at the oncoming crowd growing larger with each passing moment. He had missed out on two opportunities for a better life—now a third was being offered him. But a lawman—a deputy? He'd never dreamed such would come to pass, but maybe Sam Avery was right—maybe he did have the makings.

"I'm willing," he said, and let it drop there, economical, as always, with words.

The publishers hope that this Large Print Book has brought you pleasurable reading. Each title is designed to make the text as easy to see as possible. G. K. Hall Large Print Books are available from your library and your local bookstore. Or you can receive information on upcoming and current Large Print Books and order directly from the publisher. Just send your name and address to:

G. K. Hall & Co.
70 Lincoln Street
Boston, Mass. 02111

or call, toll-free:

1-800-343-2806

A note on the text
Large print edition designed by
Lyda Kuth.
Composed in 18 pt English Times
on an EditWriter 7700
by Cheryl Yodlin of G.K. Hall Corp.